KU-486-554

Prisoner of Taos

Helen Lobdell

Prisoner
of
Taos

Abelard-Schuman

London New York Toronto

© Copyright 1970 by Helen Bernice Lobdell
Library of Congress Catalogue Card Number: 72-95139
Standard Book Number: 200.71640.9

An Intext Publisher

London	New York	Toronto
Abelard-Schuman	Abelard-Schuman	Abelard-Schuman
Limited	Limited	Canada Limited
8 King St. WC2	257 Park Ave. S.	1680 Midland Ave.

Printed in the United States of America

Contents

Prisoner of Taos

1

Routine Patrol

The little company of soldiers cantered across the plaza in front of the Governor's Palace, down the hard-baked sloping ground to the bridge which crossed the Little Santa Fe, and headed northward. Behind them lay the small adobe town of Santa Fe, peaceful in the sharp morning sunshine. Ahead, the trail dipped and climbed and coiled among the rolling hills and through the canyons and arroyos which stretched, blue and purple and red and tawny brown, for miles upon miles.

It was early enough to be cool and the soldiers and their mounts both felt the stimulation of the brisk breeze and crisp air. As the sun climbed higher in the blue New Mexican sky, the day would become warmer until man and beast would slow down and feel each movement an intolerable effort. But at the moment the whole atmosphere was perfect.

It was especially perfect as far as one of the soldiers was

concerned. He was Estevan Raphael Isidiro y Algadonez and he was not really a soldier at all. He was the only son of Don Ramon y Algadonez, owner of one of the largest haciendas in New Mexico. If it weren't for the fact that Lieutenant Chavez was Estevan's cousin and had happened to stop by the Hacienda Algadonez the day before yesterday and mention that the governor was shorthanded, Estevan would not be here.

Lieutenant Chavez had been talking to Don Ramon while Estevan stared moodily out of the tall window into the open courtyard where two kitchen girls were kneeling in the sun, grinding corn on their flat stone *metates.* Estevan was bored.

"We have a patrol to go on—up to San Juan," Lieutenant Chavez said, "but with one group at Taos and another off to Jemez to track down the murdering Indians who attacked the Hacienda Ulibarri, the governor is short of men."

"He is always short of men," Don Ramon said. "A pity the viceroy at Mexico City gives so little thought to our outpost here in New Mexico."

Estevan turned from the window, an idea forming in his mind.

"Si," Chavez took another drink from the wine cup he held. "Governor Otérmin has asked repeatedly for more men. The few he has been sent are boys or criminals who have no real wish to be soldiers."

"And out of such, Otérmin is to defend all of New Mexico," Don Ramon remarked. He shook his head. "It is hard to understand."

Estevan moved toward his father. "Yes, Estevan?" his father said, giving him permission to speak.

"Father, could I not volunteer to go on that patrol to

San Juan?" Estevan turned to his cousin. "The governor would accept a volunteer for one patrol, would he not?"

Chavez nodded.

"You?" Don Ramon set his cup upon the huge carved table which was his desk. "But why, my son?"

"Because I've never been ten miles from the hacienda!" Estevan burst out. "Because I have nothing to do. Please, Father?"

He turned to Chavez. "You would put in a word for me, wouldn't you?"

"With pleasure, if your father has no objections."

Don Ramon looked at his son. The boy was restless, it was true. Since he had finished lessons with Father Andres he had had little to do. He must be put to work on the hacienda. It was high time Estevan began learning his responsibilities. How old was he? Sixteen? Yes—sixteen this coming August. How fast a son grew! Why, it was only yesterday that he used to take the little fellow up on his saddle before him and ride around the hacienda. . . . Don Ramon realized that both young men were waiting for his reply.

"Why, I suppose it would do no harm," he said slowly. "It would be good for you to see the country and if it is only a routine patrol. . . ." He looked at Lieutenant Chavez.

"It is, sir. We are to check with the padre and bring back some orphans."

"Very well. Estevan has my permission."

Thus it was that Estevan was riding along with the company this fine May morning, wearing a breastplate and helmet, a leather shield slung at his saddle, the sword his father had given him for his fourteenth birthday heavy at his side. Routine patrol it was, but each man went well armed.

It was late afternoon when the little cavalcade, Lieutenant Chavez in the lead, rode into San Juan Pueblo. Built upon the bank of the Rio Chama, San Juan had been the first habitation for the Spaniards in New Mexico. Oñate and his men had taken over the main building and forced the Indians to move out until the Spaniards had built dwellings for themselves farther south.

In the large cool square of shade cast by the pueblo walls, most of the San Juan Indians were gathered, the men resting after their morning's hunt, the women weaving or grinding corn or gossiping together. Children played quietly.

All activity stopped when the Spaniards rode in. Men and women stared impassively at the visitors. Children left their games and edged toward their mothers and fathers. The only sounds were the clink of harness metal and the rushing of the Rio Chama, swollen with the melting mountain snows as it hurried past the pueblo.

As the men sat their horses and looked around, a brown-robed Franciscan priest came from the small adobe church and moved across the plaza toward them.

"*Buenos dias*, Padre," Lieutenant Chavez greeted the churchman.

"*Buenos dias*, Senor," the priest replied. Shading his eyes against the sun, he looked up at the lieutenant. "To what do we owe the pleasure of your visit?"

"Just a routine patrol," the lieutenant replied, swinging down from his saddle. "We will stay the night."

"You are welcome, Senor," the priest said, but even Estevan noted that there was no warmth in the good father's voice, only a cool, guarded politeness. He wondered about it as he climbed wearily from his horse. One would think that a man exiled to a Godforsaken spot like this would be happy to see visitors who could give him news of the outside world.

The lieutenant motioned imperatively to a group of men sitting nearby. "Here," Chavez ordered, "take our horses and see that you rub them down carefully.

"Gonzales," he said, turning to one of his soldiers, "you oversee them."

The men moved forward. They did not hesitate, but neither did they hurry and there was something in the deliberation of their movements which was disturbing to Estevan. He gave himself a mental shake. He was tired. And he had always known the Indians were resentful of the Spaniards despite all that his people had done for them.

Chavez was giving orders. "Sanchez, you and Baca take a look in the storerooms. Alvero and Sedillo, look to the fields. Algadonez, come with me."

Estevan followed his cousin toward the church. For the next hour he and Chavez went over Father Cristobal's records filling out a report for Governor Otérmin on births, deaths, acreage planted with corn, and the amount of trading with other pueblos. When the accounting was finished, Chavez leaned back in his chair.

"Six deaths," he commented. "And that leaves only three orphans?"

The priest nodded.

"Come, Father. Are you sure you are not concealing something from me?" Chavez asked. His tone was pleasant, but there was an edge of steel to it.

Father Cristobal looked blandly at the soldier. "My son, why should I withhold anything from the governor's patrol?"

Chavez laughed grimly. "Because we not only have to fight the Indians from time to time to hold New Mexico, but we carry on a constant warfare with their allies, the Franciscans," he said. "But no matter. We shall take a tally tomorrow. Come, Estevan, let me show you the pueblo where our great-grandfather once spent a winter."

"You and your men will take dinner with me?" Father Cristobal asked politely.

"*Si*, thank you, Father. We will be most happy to."

As he and his cousin sauntered around the pueblo, Estevan was uncomfortably aware of the cold hostility of the Indians. There were Indian slaves at the hacienda and there were always Indians coming into Santa Fe to trade, but this was Estevan's first experience with them on their own territory and he was startled by the strength of their feeling. What right did they have to feel that way, he wondered, when the Spaniards had come in and brought them the true faith and showed them how to farm and raise sheep and work with metal? What right did they have to be so ungrateful?

He voiced his thoughts to Lieutenant Chavez. His cousin looked at him quizzically. "You have led too sheltered a life, Kinsman," he said. "I have my job to do and the Indian is obviously created inferior to the Spaniard. But I do not wonder at his hostility. Even a horse may resent the lash."

"Even a horse may resent the lash." The remark stayed with Estevan that night as he lay rolled in his blanket beneath the bright stars. The unaccustomed hardness of his bed and the excitement of the day made him wakeful and Chavez' phrase rang in his ears. Were the Indians treated with undue cruelty? He had read accounts of Oñate's killing of the Indians, the massacre at Ácoma and such incidents, but that was only

14

because it was necessary. He had seen Indians whipped in the plaza at Santa Fe, their hands tied to posts, their backs dripping blood. And at the Hacienda Algadonez the overseer, Manuel, used the lash for disobedience. But Spanish servants, too, were whipped. It was the way of the world. It should not be the basis for hate. Estevan felt for his sword beside him and wondered if it would not be wise to stay awake in case of attack.

The next thing he knew he was being shaken roughly by one of the other soldiers. "Time to be up," the fellow said. "We are to be in saddle by sunrise."

Estevan groaned as he sat up. The long day in the saddle and sleeping on the ground combined to make him ache in every joint. As he creaked into action he was aware of his cousin's amused glance.

"You should join the army, Cousin," Chavez said to him. "You are soft from too easy a life."

Estevan buckled on his sword. "You are right," he said mournfully. "I didn't know how soft until this hour."

"Another good long day in the saddle will help," Chavez grinned as he turned to the Indian who had brought their horses. "Hold them," he directed the Indian.

"Estevan, go and tell Father Cristobal that I wish all the Indians and their children lined up in the courtyard immediately."

When Estevan delivered the message, the priest inclined his head. "It will be as the lieutenant wishes," he said coldly and gave the order to a servant who was cleaning the hearth.

When the population of San Juan was gathered in the courtyard, Lieutenant Chavez strode before them. For a long time he looked at the little family groups who stood sullenly in the gray light of dawn.

"Now, Father," he said sternly, turning to the priest, "either you designate which of these hordes of children are orphans or I'll go down the line and take every fifth child. You and I both know that all this past year you have been failing to deliver your orphaned children for care in Santa Fe."

"Care!" the priest all but spat the word. "You mean for slavery!"

"The law is the law," Chavez said evenly. "And the law says that orphaned Indians must be given into the governor's custody for care and Christian upbringing. Now, do you obey me or shall I take the children at random?"

"You could not. You would not dare!" Father Cristobal protested.

"Do you wish to see whether I dare or not?" Chavez asked. "My orders are to bring *all* of the orphans this time."

For a minute the two men measured each other.

"Gonzales," Chavez directed a grizzled, black-bearded veteran, "line up the children."

Gonzales moved to obey.

"No—wait," the priest said, defeated. "I will get the orphans."

He stepped closer to the people and spoke to them in the Teres language of the northern Pueblos. When he finished there was an angry murmur, then one woman began to wail. Others took up the cry and the sound echoed eerily through the rising river mists.

"Mount and be prepared for action," Chavez directed his men.

His heart thumping, Estevan mounted his horse. And this was a routine patrol!

"Well?" Chavez asked Father Cristobal.

"They will give them up," the priest said sadly. "Let them have the comfort of their tears for a moment."

And it was as he said. One by one, children were brought forward until ten of them stood before Lieutenant Chavez.

One little girl was brought up by a young woman who dropped upon her knees in front of the officer. Holding the child tightly and with tears streaming down her cheeks, she poured forth a torrent of words.

"She says this is her sister's child. The little girl's parents and this woman's two babies died last winter of the fever. She begs to be allowed to keep this little one," the priest said entreatingly.

"The law is the law," Chavez repeated brusquely. "The child must go to Santa Fe with the others."

Gently, the priest raised the woman and pulled her away from the child, speaking to her in her own tongue. When she understood, she flung herself from Father Cristobal and ran, sobbing, into the pueblo.

One of the Spanish two-wheeled carts had been hitched to a soldier's horse. "Put the little ones into the *carreta*," Chavez directed. "The bigger ones can walk. Algadonez and Baca, you fall in line behind the cart in case any of them decide to straggle."

As the cavalcade was forming, a tall young man came forward and taking the band from his head placed it around the head of the biggest of the orphans, a boy who looked nearly Estevan's age. The Indian said something and there was love in his eyes. Estevan looked away and felt shame in his heart for the first time in his life. The boy replied to his friend, his voice low but steady. The man patted the boy's shoulder and then stepped back.

As the soldiers moved off with the orphans, a tall man emerged from the pueblo and stood watching the scene. His figure loomed gaunt against the sky and the fierceness of his hatred boiled up within him until his eyes burned with the feel of it. El Popé lifted his arms to heaven. It was not quite time yet. But it would be soon. By all of the Kachinas in Blue Lake, it would be soon!

Lieutenant Chavez' patrol did not get back to Santa Fe that night. Encumbered with the orphans, they had to move more slowly than before. They were not much beyond San Ildefonso Pueblo when darkness overtook them. Chavez ordered camp made in the lee of a giant crag of rock, fires built, and corn pudding made for everyone. He directed that the older orphans' ankles be tied, but their hands left free until after they had eaten. The little girl began to cry and was hushed fiercely by an older child.

"Lieutenant," Estevan asked, "have we any blankets for the children?"

"Blankets—for them?" Chavez shrugged. "They are tough little animals. They don't need blankets. See to the bonds on the older ones and don't be such a duenna!"

Estevan flushed at the reprimand and went to check the boys' wrists and ankles. The biggest one was lying upon his side and pretending to be asleep, but he flinched away from Estevan's touch. "I'm sorry," Estevan wanted to say, and was ashamed that he should feel so when it was only an Indian.

Estevan rolled up in his blanket and tried to sleep. The night air was chill. It grew very cold here in the high plateaus as soon as the sun went down. He tried to sleep but kept thinking of those children in the cart. The little one was whimpering again. Finally, he could stand it no longer. Cautiously, he raised himself up on one elbow. The camp was completely quiet except for the subdued crying of the child. The guard was sitting, his back against a rock, gazing back over the route they had traveled that day. Estevan arose and, moving as stealthily as if he were an Indian himself, gathered up his blanket and went over to the cart. The little girl, huddled against an older child who was sleeping, gazed up at him, her great dark eyes shining in the moonlight. Estevan spread his blanket over the children and tucked it around the little one's shoulders.

As he settled in his place again, Estevan felt the gaze of someone upon him. He turned to look directly into the eyes of the Indian boy. Turning his back on him and wrapping his arms about his chest, he tried not to think how cold he was.

For a long time the Indian boy, Teri, stared into the dying firelight until at last he, too, fell asleep.

2

A New Body Servant

Nothing was said the next day about the children having a blanket except that when Estevan sneezed during the breaking of camp, Lieutenant Chavez remarked, "A pity you aren't as tough as the Indians."

Estevan looked after his cousin's figure and was glad he had not said more.

This third day on the trail was more difficult than either of the other two. The wind sprang up at dawn and continued all day. It shrieked through the canyons and swept across the mesas, whipping the powdery red sand into stinging clouds which bit into the skin and gritted between the teeth and smarted the eyes. The horses were restless and hard to handle as they plodded along. Visibility was extremely limited. The world was nothing but a trail beneath their feet and a great hot, stinging, red-yellow cloud enveloping them. The children in the wagon tried pulling Estevan's blanket over their heads but would get too warm and have to sit up from time to time. The little girl started to cry again. The older children stumbled as they walked and were hard to keep in line. Once, Baca had to dismount and, cursing, yank Teri up on the trail again after the boy had slipped and fallen partway down the sloping side of a canyon. He gave him a shove which sent him sprawling into the dirt of the trail. "Now watch where you're going, you fool!" Baca admonished, adding a few more good round soldier oaths.

Lieutenant Chavez came back along the trail. "What is the trouble?" he asked.

"One of the boys slipped over the edge. Baca brought him back," Estevan explained.

Chavez, looking at the group, wondered if the boy had slipped or had gone over the edge deliberately. It would be easy to lose one in this miserable sandstorm.

"Rope the boys together," he ordered. "Then we'll be sure to have them all when we reach Santa Fe."

Baca uncoiled a heavy rope from his saddle.

"Give him a hand, Algadonez," Chavez ordered.

Reluctantly, Estevan dismounted.

Baca was already yanking one of the boys' hands into position behind his back and tying the cord.

"It would be easier for them to walk with their hands in front of them," Estevan suggested.

"*Si*, and easier for them to untie the knots if they decided to slip away," Baca grunted. "When you've been around these savages as long as I have, you don't take any chances. Here, get the next one." Baca tossed him the rope end.

Estevan had no choice but to rope the largest boy's

hands together. The Indian stood proudly, his feet thrust slightly apart, but without protest submitted to the humiliation of bonds. Estevan found his own hands wet with perspiration as he secured the heavy rope. What was the matter with him? These things had to be done. And an Indian was not like a Spaniard. He probably didn't know what shame or pride meant. I'd think nothing of roping a horse, Estevan told himself. Why does roping an Indian bother me?

The little group moved forward once more, their heads bowed against the cutting wind. But their progress was even slower than before. The rope which secured the boys was too short to give much space between them and when one stumbled, it caused the next one or two to do so and it took time for them to regain their feet and resume marching. Estevan and Baca and their charges began to fall behind the others. Finally, Baca lost his temper completely when the leading boy fell over a stone and the rest piled up in a complete tangle of rope and legs and verbal outbursts.

Baca swung from his horse. Taking the top child on the heap by the hair, he jerked him viciously to his feet, then proceeded to do the same with the next and then the next until he had them all standing. "Now," he said, "you'll stop this stupid blundering and march along as you should." To show that he meant what he said, he drew his arm back and struck the first child a brutal blow across the face with the back of his large, strong hand. The child almost fell but caught himself. He did not cry out although tears filled his eyes. Baca advanced on the next youngster.

"This is to let each of you know that we are through playing nursemaid," he said, drawing his hand back for the blow.

A New Body Servant

Estevan slid from his saddle. "Baca, no," he protested, "that is not necessary!"

Surprised, Baca held back his hand. "What do you mean?" he growled.

"You have made your point," Estevan said. "Now let us catch up with the others."

"And how do you know if I've made my point?" Baca demanded angrily. "Are you the expert on Indians around here? You're not even a soldier, so mind your own business." He moved again to strike.

"I said 'no' and I meant it!" Estevan, suddenly too angry to be aware of his recklessness, shoved Baca's hand up.

The soldier turned on Estevan in a sudden savage reflex and the blow meant for the Indian crashed into the side of Estevan's face, knocking him to the ground.

"Here, here, what is the meaning of this?" a sharp voice demanded. Estevan looked up to see Lieutenant Chavez looming up out of the swirling dust. Slowly, he got to his feet.

"It is nothing," he said briefly.

"Baca, what happened?"

Baca, still angry but mindful that he had struck a relative of the lieutenant's, said, "I'm sorry, sir. He was interfering with my handling of the savages and I'm afraid that I lost my temper."

Chavez looked from one to the other. "Have you anything to say, Algadonez?"

"No, sir."

"All right, mount up and let us not have any more of this. I'd like to make Santa Fe before Corpus Christi Day."

Chavez could pretty well imagine how the incident had

been provoked, but Baca was a good soldier and it was best not to make too much of the matter. In truth, Chavez thought to himself, his cousin, Estevan, was more of an innocent than he realized. He will change when he has to manage the Indians at the Hacienda Algadonez, Chavez thought grimly. You don't handle Indians with tenderness if you want to get anything out of them.

Estevan had never in his life felt as tired and dirty as he did when they arrived in Santa Fe late that evening. His face was rough with sand and his clothes were so powdered with it that they had ceased to have any color of their own and were the red gray of the lava dust. His jaw throbbed where Baca had struck him.

Wearily, he slid down from the saddle and looped his reins over the hitching post in front of the Governor's Palace.

"Algadonez, take the orphans into the Casa," Chavez directed. "Turn them over to the governor and then you will be dismissed."

"Yes, sir," Estevan said. He began to lift the younger children from the cart. "Do I untie the others, sir?" he asked.

"No, leave them together."

Estevan marshaled the bedraggled little troop into the *Casa Real*—the Governor's Palace. The coolness of the adobe building was a blessed relief after the smothering heat of the sand-filled air outside. The children were, if possible, dirtier than Estevan and the boys' legs were covered with bruises and skinned places where they had stumbled and fallen against the sharp rocks on the trail.

Governor Otérmin looked up when the soldier at the door led Estevan and his charges into the room.

"Well, well," Otérmin leaned back in his chair. "It

looks as if your first taste of soldiering was a rough one, Estevan."

"Yes, sir." Estevan managed a weak smile. He had known the governor all of his life and could imagine Otér-min and his father laughing together over the picture he made as he stood there, surrounded by the dirty Indian children.

"It wasn't a holiday, eh?"

"Not exactly, sir."

Otérmin looked at the orphans. "Humph, Chavez did better this time. Was there any trouble over these?"

"No, sir, no trouble."

"Good. Tell Captain Rael at the door to take these people over to the padres at San Miguel. We will distribute them tomorrow."

Estevan watched the tired children as they were herded out of the room, then turned again to the governor. "Your Excellency—"

"Yes?"

"How are the orphans distributed? Who gets them?"

"Oh, we have a waiting list. Senor Romero wants some for his stables, my wife needs a new kitchen girl, the alcalde mayor wants some bigger ones to work in his silver mine. There is no problem," he answered carelessly. "Why?"

"Well—" Estevan hesitated. "I need a body servant and that biggest boy was a likely looking one. But I suppose there is no chance of getting him if there is a waiting list."

"Oh, I don't know. We will be getting others from Jemez and San Ildefonso next week. I think you could have this one. We can say you earned a place on the list by your patrol duty. Pick him up tomorrow."

"Thank you, sir."

"Now I would say you need home and a bath."

"Yes, sir, I certainly do."

"All right. You are dismissed with my thanks."

As Estevan jogged slowly home in the gathering dusk, he wondered what mad impulse had made him ask the governor for that Indian boy. He wasn't at all sure that his father would welcome the idea. And when he really considered the matter, he wasn't completely certain that he wanted an Indian body servant. A husky young fellow would probably cost quite a fee. Why had he opened his mouth before he gave the matter real thought? Well, the words had been spoken and he was committed and there was nothing left but to go in tomorrow and get him.

Estevan was right in thinking that Don Ramon might not welcome the idea of taking on the Indian boy. He was completely unenthusiastic and expressed himself quite forcefully on the subject.

"Why, by all the saints in heaven, did you speak to Otérmin before you asked me?" Don Ramon demanded. He shoved his cup of chocolate away impatiently. "I give you leave to go on a patrol and you come back with an Indian slave! Why did you do it?"

"I thought—well, I need a body servant."

"And what is wrong with Jaime Chavira as your body servant? I wasn't aware that you needed more than one."

"Well—Jaime sort of works around generally and I—I thought this boy could be mine only."

"Does he speak Spanish?"

Estevan shook his head and sneezed.

26

"Does he understand it?"

"I—I don't think so."

Don Ramon thumped the table. "Fine," he said sarcastically. "Just fine. And are you prepared to teach him? Or do you want the excitement of a servant who doesn't understand any of your commands?"

Doña Magdalena spoke. "It seems to me, my dear, that there is no point in raving at Estevan. Perhaps he made a foolish request, but what is done is done. You must honor it or humiliate him before the governor. Surely," she added reasonably, "we can find work for another pair of hands around the hacienda."

"Yes, of course. You are right," Estevan's father grunted. "Unfortunately, although my son has the look of a man, he hasn't the judgment of one. But I'll back him on this. I think I'll ride in with him, though, just in case he gets tenderhearted and decides to bring all ten of the orphans back with him!"

Estevan flushed. "I'm not that foolish, Father."

"Don't add impertinence to stupidity," Don Ramon snapped. "Be ready to leave within the hour. I have some matters to go over with Senor Manuel and then I'll be free."

So it was that Don Ramon preceded his son into Santa Fe that morning. It was a gloomy ride. Estevan's head was completely stuffed up with a cold and he felt miserable and wished bitterly that he had never heard of Indian orphans.

Nor did things improve when they reached Santa Fe. It was market day and the plaza in front of the Casa Real was full of Indians and Spaniards alike, doing a brisk business with each other. Even the wide porch of the Governor's Palace was thronged with Indians, their wares spread out on blankets

27

or displayed in baskets. The heat and the confusion did nothing to improve Don Ramon's temper or Estevan's head cold.

"I'm going into the Casa," Don Ramon said. "You go over to San Miguel and bring the boy to me."

"*Si*, Father." Estevan turned and walked his horse slowly across the plaza out to the edge of town where the Church of San Miguel stood. This church was the first in Santa Fe, far less grand than the more fashionable churches of St. Francis or Our Lady of Guadalupe.

Crossing the river and reaching the little church with its walled-in yard, Estevan looped his horse's reins over a mesquite bush in the shade of the building and went in. The churchyard was given over mainly to graves. In some cases the little wooden crosses stood straight and true in the red adobe clay, but in more they had loosened and begun to list and sag, giving the yard a dejected air.

Estevan went to the side door which led to the padre's living quarters and knocked. The three priests of Santa Fe served all the churches, but Father Andres Duran spent most of his time at San Miguel. He served a small parish which was so entirely Indian that San Miguel had come to be called the Indians' church.

Admitted by the housekeeper, Estevan waited a few minutes in the dark, sparsely furnished room which was the priest's study.

When Father Andres appeared and Estevan told him his errand, the priest was pleased. "I am happy that Teri is going to your hacienda," he said. "He is too good a boy to be worked to death in the mines."

"His name is Teri?" Estevan asked.

"Yes. He is fifteen years old and has been taken care

of, since his parents' death of the pox two years ago, by Nicholas Bua, War Chief of San Juan. And a pity he could not have been left there," the priest added bitterly. "But if he had to be brought in I'm glad, at least, to know that he will be in a good place."

When Teri was brought out, he looked once at Estevan and then kept his eyes fixed upon the floor while Father Andres made out the necessary custody papers for Don Ramon to sign.

When the papers were ready, Father Andres put his hand upon the Indian boy's shoulder. "God go with you, my son," he said in the language of the Pueblo.

Teri looked up at the priest for a moment, but did not reply. Turning, he followed Estevan out into the bright sunlight.

In the confusion of the plaza, Estevan decided that it was much safer if the Indian walked ahead of him. He motioned his wish to the boy, then mounted his horse and rode slowly, Teri preceding him, through the thronging people and yapping dogs, over to the Casa Real. As they were about to enter the Casa, there was a roll of drums, the double doors of the building swung back and a detachment of soldiers marched out with three Indians, their hands tied behind them, in their midst. Their disciplined faces impassive, the soldiers walked their prisoners to the center of the plaza, the way opening silently before them. At the whipping post the Spanish officer in charge of the detail halted the group and had one of the prisoners secured to the post, his wrists tied high above his head. When that was done the doors of the Casa opened again and Don de Xavier, Alcalde Mayor of Santa Fe, strode out. He was a little man, quick of movement, his shirt ruffles spotlessly white under his velvet coat. The mayor walked rapidly to the center of the plaza. For a moment he stood and faced the prisoners silently. Then, unrolling a paper in his hand, he read the charges in a loud voice.

Estevan, jostled by the crowd, did not hear distinctly, but the words "Popé," and "inciting to rebellion," rang out clearly. Was that man tied to the post El Popé, the shadowy figure whose name was whispered with foreboding by every Spaniard in New Mexico? Estevan looked again. The prisoner was a large man, taller than the Pueblos usually were, broad of shoulder and lean as a panther. He was dressed in cotton trousers and a long cotton tunic. The most noticeable thing about him was his exceptionally long heavy hair which hung down his back in two huge braids.

When the mayor finished his proclamation he turned and moved back to the Casa. The officer barked an order. A soldier stepped forward and tore the blue cotton tunic from the prisoner's back exposing his bronze skin to the bright sun and to the full agony of the lash which was immediately plied with a practiced hand by one of the other soldiers. The first blow left an angry red line across the taut skin, the second slashed through flesh, and by the tenth blow the blood was running down and staining the man's trousers. With the twelfth cut the Indian's knees buckled and his body sagged against the pole.

As the punishment continued the only sound in the plaza was the hiss and sickening impact as the whip bit into the raw quivering flesh of the Indian. Even the dogs were silent.

Suddenly, Estevan could watch no more. He had witnessed other whippings and they had made little impression upon him. But this was different. Estevan felt sickened at the sight of blood and the sound of the lash. He gave Teri a push toward the Casa door and felt a sense of relief when he stood inside the cool, dark hallway, the door shut against the sounds in the plaza.

When they found Don Ramon he looked at Teri without enthusiasm though he admitted to himself that the boy was good-looking for an Indian. "Do you still want him for a body servant?" he asked Estevan.

"Yes, Father." At the moment Estevan couldn't care less about a body servant. What he wanted was his home and bed and something hot to drink. But he would die before he would admit to his father that he regretted his request.

"Very well. You had better start for the hacienda. It will be a long journey and you will have to gear your horse to the boy's pace as he walks alongside. I'll be along later."

As Estevan and Teri went past the governor's office they could hear voices raised in anger. Estevan recognized the governor's roar as well as the shriller tones of the alcalde mayor.

Estevan did not look toward the center of the plaza as he swung into his saddle and directed Teri down the street to the road north from town. Teri walked swiftly and they were soon on the outskirts of Santa Fe. But it seemed to Estevan that he could hear the hiss and crack of the soldier's whip long after they had left the city behind them.

3

The Name Day

In the weeks that followed, Estevan had cause many times to reflect upon the consequences of his rash impulse. For though the boy, Teri, proved docile enough, he seemed incredibly slow to learn. And Don Ramon made it clear that it was up to Estevan to teach him. He need expect no help from anyone else at the hacienda.

Language was the first problem. Estevan could speak and understand a little of the language of the northern Pueblos but he felt it was Teri's place to speak and understand Spanish. The boy apparently knew none at all. Estevan started with the simplest words, speaking them slowly and showing Teri what they referred to. But many was the time when he ordered the boy to bring him a shirt and received, instead, a pair of boots or a doublet or hat. The worst problem was over the more abstract things—hot or cold, up and down. But Estevan felt that he was making progress by the end of two weeks and decided that he would have Teri give him his bath. It was that experience which showed him just how slow a process educating an Indian could be.

When a Spanish gentleman wished to take a bath, a large leather tub with well-calked seams was placed in his room. A little warm water was poured into the tub and the gentleman climbed in and soaped himself up. Then a servant sluiced him down with more hot water. It was a somewhat laborious process and for this reason many Spanish gentlemen—and ladies, too—did not indulge themselves in bathing any more often than was absolutely necessary. But Doña Magdalena was a great believer in cleanliness and her household bathed sometimes as often as once a week. There were plenty of servants to haul the buckets of water from the huge kitchen hearth to the private apartments and then to empty and scrub out the leather tub. Baths were no real hardship, therefore.

Estevan instructed Teri carefully in the ritual of the bath. He had the boy bring four buckets: two of boiling hot water, one of cold and an empty one to mix in. He showed him how to mix the two together to prepare a nice warm combination for the washing down. "Do you understand?" he asked, when he had finished.

Teri nodded. That should not have reassured Estevan because Teri always nodded. But it did. Esteven undressed, climbed into the tepid water he had had Teri put into the tub and soaped himself. "All right, now pour the bucket of warm water over me," he directed.

Teri, at his back, picked up a bucket and holding it over Estevan's head poured it out with a rush. A great flood of steaming water, hot enough to cook an egg, cascaded over

Estevan's head and shoulders. He let out a roar of startled pain and rage. "Not the hot, you dog, the warm!" he bellowed, "the warm!"

Naturally, that rattled the poor boy. He grabbed the next nearby bucket and obligingly threw that over his enraged master. Unfortunately that bucket contained ice-cold water. This time the shock left Estevan, for the moment, speechless. Then, with deliberation, he climbed out of the tub and stood, dripping and furious, on the cool tile floor of his room.

"You stupid fool!" he said to Teri. "You stupid, blundering fool! Why I didn't let you go to the silver mines, I'll never know. Maybe it isn't too late yet. Now, get out! Get out before I kick you all the way to the Sangres!" And Estevan took his body servant by the nape of his neck and thrust him out of the door with such violence that the boy landed on the floor of the passageway.

Teri picked himself up, looked for a moment at the closed door of his master's apartment, a little smile quirking the corner of his mouth, then turned and walked jauntily down the passageway.

The next week, Jaime Chavira assisted Estevan with his bath.

June came and went and July settled in with heat so intense that the sky seemed a huge, hot, blue bowl pressed down over the land. The work of the hacienda stopped at noon and did not resume until late afternoon, master and servants alike taking a long siesta during the oppressive midday heat. Don Ramon began to use Estevan in the business of the ranch, putting him in the charge of Manuel, the overseer, to learn the things that the master of a hacienda should know. The intricacies of the irrigation system, the problems of handling the men, the keeping of accounts, the care of the livestock—these were all vastly more complicated than Estevan had realized.

Estevan found learning the operation of the hacienda interesting and challenging although he did not care very much for Manuel. The Spanish overseer was a large, heavyset man with huge *mustachios* that drooped over the corners of his mouth. He always carried a whip in his hand and was, it seemed to Estevan, far too ready to use it on any worker who seemed to be lagging at his task.

But when Estevan spoke of this to Don Ramon, his father shook his head.

"Senor Manuel is a good man, the best I have had, Estevan," he said. "He knows how to keep the workers in line and how to get the work done. The whip is necessary, and he does the people no real injury."

"It seems to me that there are times when a command would do as well as the whip," Estevan replied.

"You don't know these people. The Indians are lazy and reluctant. They mistake kindness for weakness. You should realize that from your experience with Teri. A good lashing or two would help him to learn much faster. And with rumors of unrest among the Indians, a strong hand is needed now more than ever."

"Perhaps you are right," Estevan sighed.

"You are too gentle, my son. It takes a certain ruthlessness for the Spaniard to rule in an alien, hostile land. Father Andres has filled your head with the benign talk of the priest."

"Is such talk, then, but lies?"

"No, not lies," Don Ramon replied. "It is merely that

the priests, as men of God, are not practical. They are sincere and I'll confess that it is good for us to have them and their teachings among us to mitigate the deeds of some rancheros who would be unduly cruel. But we cannot tame New Mexico with their teachings alone."

Don Ramon's argument was reasonable and Estevan resolved to be more firm with Teri, not dreaming how easily he, too, would use the whip.

The incident came about as a result of Estevan's Name Day gift from Don Ramon. St. Estevan's Day was the third of August and Don Ramon had promised Estevan a new mount for this, his sixteenth Name Day. Horses were a passion among young Spanish gentlemen and although Estevan had the pick of his father's large stable whenever he wished, he had no particular horse of his own and it had become a source of humiliation to him. When his friends, Carlos Romero or the Otéro brothers, raced their horses or bragged of their prowess, Estevan felt at a disadvantage. It was all well and good that Don Ramon had fine Arabians but it sounded lame and childish to say, in the heat of argument, "My father's horse can beat yours!" Estevan had looked forward with eager anticipation to the day when he could say to the others with fine arrogance, "*My* horse can make yours look like a tired mule."

When the day finally came and Don Ramon had his gift brought into the patio, Estevan could not believe his eyes. The stallion which stood snuffling softly and pawing the ground with a graceful foreleg was the most magnificent beast he had ever seen. Glistening black and shining in the sun, its neck arched and eye proud, the horse was everything a young man might dream of. Don Ramon had included as part of the gift a fine moroccan-leather saddle, silver trimmed, and as handsome a specimen of its kind as the horse itself.

For a moment, Estevan found himself speechless. Then, with a heartfelt, "Oh, Father!" he leaped up from the breakfast table that was set in the shade near the patio wall and ran over to the horse.

The animal, nervous and high-strung, reared at Estevan's approach and Pedro, the stable man, had difficulty holding the reins.

"Softly, softly, Galante," Pedro soothed. "You must not fear your new master."

Galante—a *perfect* name. Estevan checked himself and approached the horse more slowly. Gently, he reached up and patted Galante's cheek, speaking to the animal in a low voice.

The horse seemed to know that there was nothing to fear, and calmed down at once.

"Here, Senor Estevan, this will help." Pedro held out a lump of sugar.

Estevan took it in his palm and held it up to Galante's nose. Gently, the stallion nuzzled Estevan's palm and then took the sugar.

Estevan chuckled. "You beauty," he said. "Oh, you beauty!" The horse nudged Estevan's shoulder as if to acknowledge the compliment.

The youngster turned a radiant face toward his parents who had been watching from the breakfast table. "May I ride him now?" Estevan asked.

"Of course, my son. He is yours," his father replied.

Estevan took the reins from Pedro and, speaking softly to Galante, moved around to the left side of the animal. He patted the horse's neck where his silken hair, brushed until it glistened, hung heavy. Galante's ears twitched but he stood quietly.

Estevan put a foot into the stirrup and swung himself into the saddle. Leaning forward, he patted Galante again and said, "Now, let us get acquainted, you and I."

Responding to the pressure of Estevan's knee against his side and the pull of the rein, Galante wheeled and trotted obediently out of the patio and through the postern gate. Crossing the stable yard, the horse skirted the kitchen gardens and moved down the gentle slope to the dry riverbed. Estevan noted with incredulous delight the smoothness of Galante's pace and the comfort of the new saddle. Wait until Carlos Romero saw this!

Across the river the land lay smooth, rising finally to the peaks and canyons of the Sangres. It was early and the morning breeze was cool. Estevan decided that it would not be harmful to Galante to test what the animal could do.

The boy leaned forward and spoke to the horse, urging him to move faster. Galante obeyed and before he knew it, Estevan felt that he was flying, so smoothly and swiftly did the animal cover the desert stretch. A startled jackrabbit looked up in time to see the pounding hooves flash past. Two prairie dogs ducked out of the way and scurried into their burrows. Estevan gave Galante the bit and let the horse go as fast as he wished for a few minutes. Enjoying his new freedom as much as his master, the animal became one with the wind.

Reluctantly, Estevan finally curbed Galante. He did not want to stop, but he did not wish to overheat his mount either, for the sun was already blazing across the land.

The Name Day

Galante responded obediently and rider and horse turned and cantered slowly back to the hacienda. As Estevan dismounted at the stable and handed the reins to Pedro he said, "Rub him down well, Pedro. He's the most perfect horse in the world and deserves the best of care."

"*Sí*, Senor, *sí*," Pedro replied, smiling broadly, his large white teeth gleaming in the sunlight.

For a few moments Estevan lingered, reluctant to leave Galante, even briefly. At last, he tore himself away. As he ran back to the patio to tell his father how exceptional and magnificent a creature Galante was, he did not notice Teri crouched in the corner of the stable yard.

Teri had watched Estevan ride off on Galante and then return, and a longing and bitterness had arisen within the Indian boy that seemed like a clenched fist inside his ribs. Why should it be that only the Spaniards could ride horses? Why, the fist demanded, could not Teri ever hope to sit astride a beautiful animal like that?

A dozen times that day, Estevan stopped by the stables to see Galante. It was only with the greatest difficulty that Doña Magdalena drove him to his room to take his siesta. "You will not be fit for your party tonight," she scolded, "if you do not rest. That precious horse will survive without seeing you for two hours!"

"Perhaps, my dear," Don Ramon jested, "you had better check and make sure Estevan does not take the horse to *bed* with him."

"It wouldn't surprise me at all," Doña Magdalena sputtered. "Now, go, Estevan."

Reluctantly, Estevan went down the hall to his room. He had thought this would be a fine time to take Galante into

39

the shade of the stable yard and start teaching him a few tricks.

Lying on the high bed in his darkened, cool room, Estevan tried to sleep but he could not. Through his mind raced all kinds of delightful pictures—the surprise and awe of his friends: Carlos Romero, Juan and Felipe Otéro and all the others; the races Galante would win for him; long days roaming the countryside astride his mount.

The rumpled bed grew intolerable and at last Estevan sat up. He swung his feet down to the cool floor and reached for his jacket and boots. Siestas were fine but not on this day, not when out in the stable he had the finest horse in all of New Mexico!

With his high leather boots in his hand, Estevan tiptoed quietly across the room and out to the patio. He stopped at a bench in the corner to pull on his boots before going out to the stables.

Running across the stable yard, he entered the building and hurried over to Galante's stall. After the blinding glare of the New Mexico midday sun, Estevan found the stable so dark that for a moment he was completely blinded. He spoke without seeing. "Ah, my Galante, are you taking a siesta also? See, I have brought you a sweet. Come—"

Then, as his eyes became more accustomed to the darkness, Estevan could see that Galante was not in his stall. The boy's heart pounded in sudden fright. Had something happened to his horse? Had someone failed to close the stall door? Was Galante lost?

"Pedro, wake up! Galante is gone!" Estevan called excitedly.

Suddenly, he heard a whinny and the sound of hooves on the adobe clay of the stable yard. Running back to the door, he was just in time to see Teri pull Galante to a stop and slide silently off the horse's back.

For a second, Estevan stared, unbelieving. An Indian riding a horse was against the law and punishable by whipping or even death. Horses belonged to Spaniards and to them alone. To have a slave mounted on any horse was effrontery enough, but for that horse to be Galante was. . . . All the frustrations and irritations of his previous encounters with Teri came to the surface now and, combined with his reaction to this most monstrous deed of all, caused a sudden blind fury to grip Estevan. Almost without thinking, he seized a whip which hung on a peg in the wall and strode out to where the young Indian was slipping the bridle off over Galante's head.

"Stand away from that horse," Estevan ordered, his voice shrill with anger.

Teri looked up, his face expressionless save for a flicker in his dark eyes as he took in the significance of the angry young man who confronted him. He dropped the reins of the horse.

Pedro, awakened from his siesta, came out of the barn. "What is it, Senor? What has happened?"

"I have an Indian here who needs to be taught his place," Estevan said grimly, "and I intend to do the teaching. Take Galante."

Pedro picked up Galante's trailing reins and led the horse back to his stall. Teri did not move or speak. He had known the danger of riding that horse and yet there was something inside him which compelled him to risk any punishment for the sake of being astride, just once, such a magnificent beast.

Teri stared at the arrogant young Spaniard who was lifting the whip to strike and suddenly hated him. Who did these Spaniards think they were, to enslave his peoople and treat them like dogs? Why should not he, Teri, ride a horse if he wished—

The whip hissed through the air and bore down forcefully on Teri's shoulders, cutting through the rough cotton of his shirt. The Indian could feel its tip flick against his cheek, breaking the skin and causing it to bleed. But he gave no sign. Four times the whip descended across the boy's body.

Finally, Estevan threw it aside. "That is only a taste of what you'll get if you ever so much as *touch* Galante again," he said and strode away.

As he reentered the patio, Estevan met his father. "Who was the horseman I heard?" Don Ramon asked.

When Estevan explained, Don Ramon turned without a word and strode out to the stable. "Pedro," he demanded, "bring the Indian to me."

Don Ramon was as appalled at the boldness of Teri's act as Estevan had been. Things were coming to a pretty pass, indeed, if Indians were looking upon horses for themselves. That's what came of Otérmin's coddling the savages. A stronger hand and they would know their place. What we need here, Don Ramon thought to himself, is an oñate to curb them. *He* knew how to deal with Indians!

Teri was shoved forward.

"Tie him to the post," Don Ramon ordered.

As the boy's wrists were bound and secured, a crowd of stable and farmhands gathered, attracted by the unusual amount of noise during siesta.

"Find Senor Manuel," Don Ramon ordered one of the men.

"Senor," Don Ramon said when the overseer appeared,

"this Indian took it upon himself to test my son's horse. Punish him as you see fit. Make sure that not only he but others like him know that it is not for Indians to ride horses."

Senor Manuel uncoiled his rawhide whip and stepped forward. On his face was an expression that sickened Estevan. For it was not only pleasure that he saw, but a self-righteousness which made the overseer's task almost a holy one to him.

Estevan, his anger at Teri somewhat appeased, realized with horror that this beating Manuel was about to give would probably mean the boy's life. His father's command left it up to Manuel. And Manuel was going to be thorough. Of that there was no doubt. Had he, Estevan asked himself, saved Teri from the silver mines only to be the cause of his agonizing death from the overseer's lash?

Estevan turned and hurried after his father. Don Ramon had seated himself in the patio beneath an olive tree which grew against the wall.

"Yes, Estevan, what is it?" Don Ramon asked as his son stood before him. He ran his hand over his forehead. The day was, in truth, a hot one.

"Father, let me stop the punishment of the Indian."

"Why, my son?"

Estevan hesitated. He could hear the sound of the whip. "I don't know, sir, except that I feel responsible for Teri and it is my Name Day and I hate to have the blood, even of an Indian, on my hands on this day."

"Why do you consider it on your hands?" Don Ramon asked.

"I never would have known about the ride had I taken my siesta."

Don Ramon laughed. "Your logic hardly does credit to

43

Father Andres' teachings," he said. "But I can see your point. All right, stop Manuel whenever you see fit."

"Thank you, Father."

"You may go."

Estevan turned and ran from the courtyard. Don Ramon smiled indulgently as he watched his son's tall figure disappear. The Indian needed a lesson, but he wouldn't spoil the boy's Name Day. There would be other days, other times.

When Estevan reached the stable yard, the whip was descending for the seventh time and Teri's shirt was badly torn and red with blood. As the whip hissed again, the boy's knees buckled and his body sagged against the post.

"Senor Manuel," Estevan said quickly, putting his hand on the overseer's arm as he poised for another strike.

"Yes, Senor Estevan?" Manuel could not hide his impatience at the interruption.

"Senor, if you please, my father has given me permission to stop the punishment."

"You know, Senor, that it should be death for the upstart. We cannot let Indians get to thinking they are as good as we are or we won't last ten more years in New Mexico."

"I know, but it is my Name Day and I would not like to see the boy die, in spite of his crime. I would show mercy this time."

The overseer shrugged and began coiling his whip. "As you wish, Senor, but it is a mistake to let them get away with anything." He looked around at the solemn faces in the stable yard.

"Do you all understand?" he demanded. "This Indian deserves death for his arrogance and he would get it but for the gracious kindliness of Senor Estevan who would not have blood shed on his Name Day."

He strode up to the body sagging against the post. Taking hold of Teri's hair he pulled the boy's head back. "Remember that," Manuel said. "Remember, you owe your life to the generosity of Senor Estevan."

Through the haze of pain and nausea which enveloped him, Teri heard the overseer's words faintly. He owed his life to Senor Estevan. Senor Estevan is making a mistake, he thought grimly. He is—but the sickness and the agony grew greater and his head was filled with the roaring of the wind and suddenly, Teri knew no more.

When Estevan began dressing that evening for his Name Day party, the *Sangre de Cristos* mountains were showing the red sunset light which gave them the name "Blood of Christ." Had Estevan looked from his window he might have seen a thin spiral of smoke ascend the quiet luminous sky from one of the lesser peaks of the Sangres. A spiral, a break, and then two more. But Estevan did not notice. He had no time to be looking out of the window. It was necessary to dress and he had no body servant to assist him.

Debating, he pulled off his boots. Perhaps Teri should be compelled to go on with his regular duties. But Estevan shrank from further encounter with him today. Instead, he went to his door and shouted, "Jaime!"

It was some time before Jaime Chavira appeared.

"It took you long enough," Estevan grumbled, unfastening his fine white shirt and pulling it off over his head.

Jaime stepped forward and took the shirt. "I'm sorry, Senor. The senora sent me on an errand and I did not know you would be wanting me." Jaime stooped and began unlacing Estevan's long hose.

Jaime Chavira, a boy of about Estevan's age, had been a

part of the Algadonez household for more than five years. His parents had been killed by a straggling band of Apaches as they journeyed to Santa Fe from the south. He and Estevan had been friends when they were little, swimming in the river, setting snares for jackrabbits and riding together when Jaime could get away from his household tasks. But that was long ago and now their lives had taken different paths: Jaime was servant and Estevan, master and the old camaraderie was forgotten. After all, the only son of one of the greatest rancheros in Nueva Mexico could hardly be friends with a mere serving boy. The idea would be as unthinkable to Jaime as it was to Estevan.

With Jaime's help, Estevan was soon ready to go and greet his guests. And handsome enough he looked, in his rich red velvet suit, the frothy lace of his shirt front spilling over the gold embroidered lapels. From the top of his curly head to the shining toes of his fine leather boots, Estevan was every inch the Don. He strode off down the corridor with the self-confident carriage and easy grace of one who had never had to do menial chores of any kind.

"Your party is a success, my son," Doña Magdalena said, coming up to Estevan. "Why are you not dancing?"

Estevan beamed down at the fragile little woman who ruled the household. "It is a wonderful party, Senora, thanks to you, and I am not dancing because I am waiting to claim Senorita Otéro."

"She is indeed lovely tonight," the senora remarked as the lady in question went whirling past, her voluminous skirts frothing about her ankles, and her lace mantilla looped gracefully over her shoulders.

Estevan claimed Senorita Isabella Otéro for the next dance and managed to keep her for his supper partner.

They ate their chicken with rice (*Pollo con arroz*) and bar-
becued meat (*asados*) as they sat on a carved bench in the
patio. The music of the three guitarists came to them muted
and quiet after the pounding rhythms of the dance, and the
stars hung close in the soft black velvet of the sky. Others
were eating in the patio also and there was the sound of
laughter and the tinkle of glass as servants moved about carrying coffee and chocolate and the soft custard dessert known
as *nantillas*.

Estevan was suddenly aware of how truly lovely Senorita Isabella was. Her face was half-lighted by the lantern
which flickered from the wall and Estevan wondered why he
had never noticed before how red her lips were and how soft
and lustrous her hair. He had known Isabella for a long
time but he had never really given her much thought before.

Isabella looked up from her plate to find him staring
at her. "What is it?" she asked. "Are you not hungry?"

"Hungry?" Estevan repeated foolishly. How long her
eyelashes were, he thought. "Oh, yes, of course." A little provoked with himself, he began eating the rice on his plate.
Why should Isabella Otéro disturb him so?

"Did you notice how many *piñon* tarts Governor Otérmin had upon his plate when he sat down to eat?" Isabella
asked.

"No, why?"

She laughed. "One assumes he likes them rather well,"
she said. "I counted six."

"Perhaps the weighty problems of office provoke an
unusual hunger for pastry," Estevan suggested.

"Or perhaps his cook always burns them and he gets
good ones only away from home," Isabella added.

The glittering lights of the innumerable candles seemed

garish as Estevan and Isabella walked back into the house. As soon as they entered the room, Isabella was borne off by a bevy of flounced and fluttering girls who just *had* to talk with her, and Estevan was hailed by Carlos Romero.

"What is this I hear about your new mount?" Carlos asked. The young man, sandy-haired and freckled, was a true Castilian with a consuming passion for horses.

"It's a beauty," Estevan answered. "It has fire and mettle and intelligence."

"Can we see him?" Carlos asked.

There was a chorus of eager enthusiasm for a visit to the stables.

"I don't know if it is safe to show a good horse to Carlos, here," Juan Otéro drawled. "He has never owned a really good one himself, you know."

There was laughter at the jibe, Carlos being known for losing many horse races.

"My mare can outrun that spavined brute of yours any day!" Carlos sputtered.

"What will you back that with?" Juan asked.

"Fifty *reales*."

"Agreed. When shall we race?"

"Tomorrow, at daybreak."

"If you want to see Galante, please excuse me while I get permission to leave," Estevan said, walking away from the group.

He could not locate his mother, but his father was standing near the hall entrance, speaking with Governor Otérmin and Father Andres.

Waiting for his father to notice him, Estevan could not help but overhear the conversation of the three men.

"Why should the Indians be upset now? Things are much better than they were forty years ago and they didn't really do anything then," Governor Otérmin was protesting.

Don Ramon nodded. "That is true," he said.

"The alcalde mayor's imprisonment and flogging of El Popé was not calculated to quiet unrest," Father Andres observed.

"But you forget that this is 1680, not 1610. The Pueblos have learned a thorough lesson these past seventy years. They know their masters. And our firm handling of wild-eyed fanatics like El Popé stops any other idea from taking root. If we handle all such cases as gently as the church would wish, we might be in for trouble!" The governor spoke with some heat.

Don Ramon noticed Estevan then and nodded for him to speak. When Estevan's request was granted he sped off to take his friends to the stable. In the excitement of showing Galante to them, Estevan forgot the conversation. It wasn't until later that he was reminded of the priest's grave words.

The party was over. The last gift had been unwrapped, the last piñon tart consumed and the remaining guests sent on their way. But Estevan was too excited to settle down for the night and decided to go out to the stable and pay Galante another visit.

The stars were bright and the moon well on the wane as Estevan walked quietly across the patio. No sound could be heard and even the servants, finished with their work for the night, had gone to their little cottages to bed.

As Estevan was about to enter the stable he was startled by a rustle in the scrubby mesquite at the corner of the building. The shadows were so dark that he could not make out any form. Was it a coyote or some other wild animal? He stared intently but there was no further sound or glimpse of anything. Just as he turned to enter the building, he saw a shadow moving across the corner of the stable yard. As the figure approached the edge of the yard and then moved off into the desert beyond, it straightened up for a moment and stood as if gazing back at the hacienda. Estevan saw that the figure was that of a human and as he remembered the conversation he had overheard earlier, he felt suddenly chilled. There was something menacing about the sight of that figure outlined against the sky, something grim and foreboding. Was there really unrest among the Indians, he wondered? Then the figure moved away and was swallowed up in the shadows, and the only sound that could be heard was the sudden scream of a shrike as it struck at its prey in the desert.

4
Journey to Taos

When Estevan awoke at dawn the next day he rolled over in bed and wished fervently that his Name Day had not been in the middle of the week. To force himself out of bed and report to Don Manuel seemed more than he could manage. If *only* this were Sunday. As he lay in bed thinking, there was a tap on his door and Jaime Chavira entered the room, carrying the usual cup of chocolate that preceded breakfast.

Grumpily, Estevan pulled himself up in bed. "Where is Teri?" he asked. The boy should be well enough this morning to perform his tasks.

Jaime set the chocolate on the stand by Estevan's bed and opened the shutters to the window. "He's gone," he said.

"Gone? What do you mean?"

"He ran away during the night."

Estevan remembered the silent, menacing figure in the

moonlight. He took a sip of his chocolate and set it down. "Has Father sent anyone after him?" he asked.

"Not that I know of, Senor." Jaime moved around the room, putting away the clothes Estevan had dropped when he undressed and went to bed in the early hours of the morning. He brought Estevan's work clothes from the curtained storage space and laid them on the bed.

Estevan threw back the covers and, leaping out of bed, began hurriedly to dress.

"Do you know where my father is?"

"He was out at the stables when I came in, Senor."

As soon as he was dressed, Estevan sought out Don Ramon. The news of Teri's flight disturbed him, not only because he represented loss of property but because, in some obscure way, Estevan felt a sense of failure with the boy. He had had only goodwill and sympathy for Teri and yet he had not been able to get through to him to establish any kind of friendliness or understanding. A master and his man-servant should share some measure of understanding and loyalty.

When Estevan located him, Don Ramon was standing near the stable door watching the stable boys go about their duties. "You haven't come out to ride Galante before breakfast, have you?" he asked his son.

"No, Father. I came to see what is to be done about Teri's disappearance."

Don Ramon shrugged. "The usual. I will send word to Otérmin and a soldier will go up to San Juan and bring him back. Governor Otérmin will have him punished as he sees fit."

"Will he be killed?" Estevan asked.

"I don't know. He will be made an example of and I

would surmise the governor will be severe. We cannot allow such actions to go unpunished if we are to keep any control of the Indians."

"Would it make a difference if we did not ask the governor to go after Teri?"

"Do you mean to let him go?" Don Ramon asked.

"No, but if we caught him ourselves."

Don Ramon considered. "It would mean that we could determine his punishment."

"And would you think it should be death?"

Don Ramon looked at his son curiously. "I cannot fathom your interest in the boy," he said, shaking his head. "He is nothing but an Indian—and, I judge, a surly malcontent at that."

Estevan did not try to explain. He could not because he did not understand his feelings himself. "Would you spare his life?" he persisted.

"Why, yes, if it means so much to you."

"Then may I go after him?"

"It is a whole day's journey to San Juan."

"I know."

"This means very much to you?"

"Yes, Father, it does."

"Very well, take Jaime Chavira with you and get started immediately. Go to the priest and explain that if he gives the boy up to you, it may save his life."

"Yes, Father. *Gracias.*"

Within the hour, Estevan and Jaime were on their way to San Juan Pueblo. The ride, though hot, was uneventful and they reached the pueblo in good time.

Father Cristobal, gravely polite, listened to Estevan's story but shook his head when he finished. "I appreciate your concern," he said, "and I would gladly try to persuade the boy to go back with you if I could. But he is not here. I have not seen him."

"But this is his home. Where else would he go?" Estevan asked.

The priest considered. "His friend, Nicholas Bua, has been in Taos for the past several weeks. Perhaps Teri went to him."

"How would Teri know Bua was in Taos if he hadn't come here first?" Estevan asked suspiciously.

Father Cristobal smiled at the boy's tone of voice. "My son, the Indians have ways of communicating with each other which put to shame the most able courier system the viceroy could ever devise," he replied.

Estevan was silent for a moment. Taos lay north and east of San Juan by about another day's journey. His parents would be concerned over his prolonged absence but if there was a chance of finding Teri at the other pueblo, he wanted desperately to go after him. Besides, the adventure of the ride farther north appealed strongly to him. They could rest here until early the next morning, go on to Taos and perhaps get home in another two days.

The priest guessed his thoughts. "If you are considering going on to Taos, Senor Estevan, I would advise strongly against it," he said.

"Why, Father?"

"Because there is much unrest among the Pueblos right now. El Popé is at Taos, still smarting from his public beating in Santa Fe two months ago. And Nicholas Bua, El Popé's son-in-law, has an interest in Teri. To go up there without any military escort and demand that Teri be given back to you might well stir up a hornets' nest that could result in some dangerous stings for you and your man."

The priest's advice fell on deaf ears. Estevan's life had conditioned him so completely to the authority and invincibility of the Spaniard that he could not conceive of any situation in which the Indians would dare to defy him openly. They might lie to him and refuse to give Teri up by deception, but for them to pose any threat of bodily danger to himself and Jaime was a preposterous idea.

"Thank you, Father. I appreciate your advice," he replied, "but I feel that we must try to get Teri without any help from the governor. If we can beg shelter of you for the night we will be on our way before dawn tomorrow."

"Of course. My house is at your disposal," the priest replied. "I am honored to have you stay with me."

The next morning, fortified with a generous breakfast provided by Father Cristobal and a map he had drawn of the route, to guide them, Estevan and Jaime were on their way north. As they cantered easily along in the brisk dawn air, Estevan felt a thrill of anticipation for the adventure that lay ahead. Taos was almost thirty leagues north of Santa Fe. It was the greatest of the pueblos, rising story upon story in the shadow of the Sacred Mountain, and it was venerated by all the Pueblos. High in the mountains nearby lay Blue Lake where the Indians believed the Kachinas, the spirits of all the Indian dead, dwelt. Father Andres had served as a priest at Taos for a short time and he had said much about the beauty of the pueblo and its legends.

Their route lay across gently rolling uplands that climbed steadily, but imperceptibly, until they were crossing a great arid plateau region dotted with scrubby bushes and scattered sage and cholla cactus. Here and there a scraggly yucca pointed its sharp spines toward the sky, its last year's flower stalk a tough brown sentinel of the plain.

By noon the boys and their mounts were both feeling the effects not only of the intense heat but of the thinner air of the higher altitude. Weary, Estevan slid from his saddle to the shade of a great outcropping of red rock. "Let us siesta until the sun drops a little," he said. "We cannot be far from Taos and we will have to spend the night there, anyway."

"As you wish, Senor." Jaime, too, was grateful for the chance to rest. He was not used to so much riding, and his legs and thighs ached.

The boys drank from their water skins and when Jaime had watered the horses and tethered them to a bit of juniper, he flung himself down beside Estevan on the hard ground.

It was almost two hours later when Estevan awoke with a start. The position of the sun told him that they had rested too long.

"Hurry," he said, shaking Jaime, "or you and I will be sleeping on the trail tonight!"

Taos was farther than Estevan had imagined and it was early dusk when the two boys, following the trail through the lower Sangres, arrived at last at a vantage point which commanded a view of the famous pueblo. The boys reined in their horses and sat looking down on the settlement. The huge bulk of the pueblo building loomed at one side while smaller buildings of various sizes and shapes were scattered on the other side of the central plaza. The golden glow of the sunset was reflected in small cookfires that dotted the scene.

Estevan wondered aloud where the priest's house would be.

Jaime pointed. "Over there. That looks like the church. The padre's house would be one of those buildings nearby."

Yes, Jaime was right. There was the church off beyond a large rounded structure that circled upward from the floor of the plaza.

There seemed to be a great deal of activity at the pueblo. Was Taos always this busy, Estevan wondered? San Juan had been very quiet in the late afternoon but here at Taos, people in great numbers were milling about and talking and there was an excitement in the air which the boys, as far from the pueblo as they were, could sense.

Estevan remembered Father Cristobal's words of warning. Was it dangerous to go down into the midst of that restless crowd of Indians and demand Teri's return? For the first time a trickle of doubt filtered through Estevan's mind. He resolved to be cautious.

"Jaime," he said, turning to the servant, "you find a sheltered spot where you won't be noticed—maybe in that arroyo over there—and keep yourself and the horses out of sight. I'm going to skirt around the plaza and look for the padre before I let myself be seen. There should be at least two or three soldiers here. I'll get them before I ask for Teri."

"As you wish, Senor." Jaime took Galante's reins as Estevan slid down from the saddle. "Be careful, Senor," he cautioned.

"*Gracias*, Jaime. I will be the soul of caution," Estevan promised.

Quietly, being careful not to dislodge any stones, Estevan worked his way down the slope of the hill. Slipping behind the circular building, he was unnoticed and was able to get over to the church without incident.

There was a light in the church. The padre would be

conducting vespers at this time of day. Estevan determined to stay out of sight until after the service when the Indians had gone, and then he would speak to the father. Stopping in the shadow of the entrance arch, Estevan looked down the nave of the church and was astounded to find it empty except for the dark-robed figure of the priest who knelt before the altar.

Where were the Indians? Surely, no matter what the excitement outside, some would be here at the evening prayers! Estevan walked slowly down the empty room.

The priest finished his prayer and rose. He turned slowly and Estevan noticed how gray and strained his face looked in the dim flickering candlelight. When the priest saw that it was a Spaniard who stood before him, he was astounded.

"My son, how did you get through the plaza?" he asked incredulously.

"I hid in the shadows and the Indians seem too excited to pay much attention," Estevan replied.

"Delegates from many pueblos meet with El Popé today," the priest said. "The rebellion of the Pueblos is about to start!"

"Rebellion?" Estevan echoed. "But that is impossible!"

"Not impossible—inevitable," the priest replied.

"Do the soldiers know?" Estevan asked.

"There are only four soldiers here, but were there forty they could not stop El Popé." The priest's voice did not sound frightened, only resigned.

Estevan found it hard to comprehend the situation. He wondered if the priest knew what he was talking about. Perhaps he had been up here too long among the Indians and mistook rumor for reality.

"Why don't you come back to Santa Fe with us?" he

asked. "I have come to get a runaway slave boy who we think is here. I'll go after him and then. . . ."

He was interrupted by a chuckle of laughter from the priest. "Ah, my son, forgive my rudeness, but we Spaniards are a breed apart. Of that, there is no doubt. Those church doors may be shattered at any moment and a howling mob of savages may break in upon us with murder in their hearts— and you stand there calmly talking about picking up a runaway slave!"

He put his hand on Estevan's arm. "Don't you realize that each moment you stand here it becomes more dangerous? It is God's miracle that you ever got here in the first place. Go—get back to your horse and fly from here as fast as you can! Get to Santa Fe and warn the governor!"

The noises in the plaza seemed to increase in volume.

"Tell the governor this is no small uprising. I have seen delegations from every pueblo in New Mexico go past my door, and even the Apache has sat at El Popé's council fire. Tell the governor to act before it is too late!"

"But why cannot you come, too?" Estevan asked, loath to leave the priest here.

"Because the Taos are my children and I will not flinch from being with them in time of danger. I cannot expect any of them to keep faith if I fail to. But get you gone and deliver my warning to the governor with all haste!"

"All right, Father." Estevan knelt for a blessing.

His heart pounded strangely as he slipped through the door and stood in the shadow of the church wall. He was both frightened and confused. This monstrous thing couldn't be happening!

By now, larger fires had been built in the plaza and flames

leaped high against the growing darkness. Voices sounded shrill and excited as the Indians gathered in greater and greater numbers. Estevan took a deep breath and plunged into the shadows.

Reaching the round building which had shielded him before, he was horrified to see coming toward him a pack of small children, screaming and brandishing sticks. After a moment of panic, he realized that they were not coming after him but were merely playing a game. He also realized that if he were to retreat around the building to keep out of their sight, he would be forced into the full view of everyone in the plaza.

Desperately he looked around. The top of the building was dome-shaped but it was above the eye level of the children and he might not be seen. It took only a second to scramble up and flatten himself out. As soon as the children were gone he would drop back down and escape. But the youngsters did not go away. They started chasing each other around the building in an endless game of tag, their shrieks and howls becoming so ear-splitting that several men came over to investigate. Estevan saw them coming and knew that he could not escape detection when they drew near. What could he do? There was no possible place of concealment. He looked around frantically.

There was a sort of chimney at the top of the dome. Perhaps, he decided, he could crouch in the shadow of that and not be seen. It was a slim chance, but the only one he had. He slithered up the curving roof to find, not a chimney, but an opening and a ladder. And suddenly Estevan realized what this building was. It was the Great Kiva of Taos, the sacred ceremonial building where the men danced and prayed to their Kachinas.

Estevan looked around. More men were coming. To stay where he was meant sure discovery. To slip down into the black depths of the kiva was risky, but at least it offered a chance. Maybe they wouldn't be using the kiva tonight and after a while, when things were quieter, Estevan could slip out again.

It took him only a second to make up his mind and, even as he was thinking, he crouched as low as he could possibly manage and slid over into the hole, feeling his way down the rough ladder in utter blackness. A strong odor assailed him as he was swallowed up in the suffocating darkness. It was an odor compounded of body sweat, animal fat, damp earth and burned-out embers.

Estevan stood on the cold, hard-packed earth at the foot of the ladder and strained his eyes to see. Presently he made out the vague shape of pillars supporting the roof and a sort of altar at one side. He moved back and began exploring around the walls. Maybe there was another opening into the room, an escape tunnel of some sort.

He had covered only a short distance when he came to a large square support which jutted out from the wall, buttressing it against pressure from the earth outside. He was about to move around the support to continue his circle when he heard the soft thud of moccasined feet on the roof over his head. Then the faint gray shadow of the opening was blacked out as a figure filled the space and began to descend the ladder.

Estevan looked around desperately. If only he could see! There might be a good hiding place nearby, but he had no way of finding it. He shrank back into the angle of the buttress, crouching low and making himself as inconspicuous as he possibly could.

A second man followed the first down the ladder and the two of them proceeded to build a fire in front of the altar block across the kiva from Estevan. Presently, a narrow, orange knife of flame slit the blackness, followed by other quivering blades of light—red, blue and yellow. Shadows leaped and played against the circular roof of the kiva as the fire grew brighter.

For a few minutes the two Indians squatted silently beside the fire, feeding it an occasional stick of piñon. The air grew heavy with smoke and the smell of the pine. Before long, the first two men were joined by other Pueblos who came down the ladder and took their places silently in a circle around the fire. As each additional Indian appeared, Estevan saw his opportunity for escape grow slimmer.

What will I do if they discover me? he asked himself. He tried to formulate a plan of action, but his mind seemed too fuzzy to face the problem. All he could do was crouch in his corner and pray that they would not build a fire large enough to penetrate the shadows around the kiva wall.

More and more Indians came. The younger ones took places toward the outer perimeter of the kiva; the more important ones, judging from their appearance and clothing, clustered near the fire. There was a murmur of conversation and then, from somewhere in the blackness beyond the altar, came the beat of a drum. The sound pulsated through the chamber as more and more men noiselessly descended the ladder.

The kiva filled and the outer circle of young men was pushed farther back toward the wall. One young fellow brushed against Estevan's knee as he went past and, through his mounting fear, Estevan found himself wondering if that might have been Teri who had passed so close and was perhaps at this moment only on the other side of the roof support. He wondered how long it would be until someone stumbled against him and looked around to discover that it was not a Pueblo crouching there.

Estevan could not know it but he had become a part of a great meeting of all the Pueblos. Not only men of Taos gathered in the Great Kiva this night, but spokesmen from San Juan, San Ildefonso, Ácoma, San Felipe and Zuni rubbed shoulders. Tupatú, of the Picuris, sat with El Saca, the Big Earring Man of Taos, and Nicholas Bua of San Juan.

A sudden silence fell upon the gathering as a figure descended the ladder and took a place behind the flames of the fire. Estevan, straining to see, found the newcomer an awesome figure, towering over the others, the flames of the fire casting flickering shadows across his stern face and highlighting the bull-horn headdress he wore. A golden animal skin girdled his waist, and heavy black braids hung down across his chest. There was something vaguely familiar about the man and suddenly Estevan recognized him as the one who had hung like a slaughtered carcass against the whipping post in Santa Fe Plaza. El Popé!

The drums had stopped beating and for a moment the only sounds were the crackling fire and slight shuffling of feet as everyone in the audience gave his full attention to the leader. El Popé's shadow danced, huge and wavering, upon the wall and ceiling behind him.

Finally El Popé drew from a pouch at his waist a great handful of sacred cornmeal and threw it on the fire. Instantly the flames died down and for a moment the kiva was in utter darkness. There was a nervous murmur until the voice of

El Popé rose in prayer to the Kachinas for guidance. As he spoke, the flames flickered upward once more and there was the illusion that they rose in response to his voice. Then, abruptly, El Popé sat down.

El Saca, the Big Earring Man, Chief of the Taos Pueblos and a strong friend of El Popé, spoke. "We have come to reach a final decision," he said. "For too long we have delayed and debated the blow which will rid us of the Spaniards and end our servitude."

There was a muttering of assent. Estevan, with his limited knowledge of the Pueblo language, could not follow all the words but he understood enough to realize their import. When there was silence again, Nicholas Bua spoke.

"It is true that we are enslaved," he said. "And I would be free again as our ancestors were, but we will pay a price for our freedom. We will lose our trade, we will loose the Apache against us once again, and we will be forced to spill the blood of the good and kindly Spaniards who have proven themselves our friends, as well as those who have plied the lash."

El Popé replied and his voice hissed through the chamber like a whip. "My son-in-law speaks with the whine of an errant maiden," he said scornfully. "There *are* no good and kindly Spaniards. The priests work their bad magic with smiling faces. They bring drought to wither our crops and plagues to kill our children. The gods they preach are their gods and work for them!"

El Popé rose and to Estevan's frightened eyes he looked ten feet tall. "We accept their puny gods and offend our Kachinas," El Popé thundered. "We are forbidden our gods and told we must worship the Spaniards'. We turn our faces from our Kachinas and then weep for our children and our crops!"

He raised his hands above the fire, which flickered low,

and began to chant. A drumbeat began softly and increased in violence as El Popé's voice rose. The smoke, the heat and the sound of the drumbeat seemed to rise and billow and intermingle until Estevan's mind became numb and his senses, dazed. And then suddenly, out of the shadows behind El Popé emerged a figure, a human figure and yet not human, that glowed and glimmered as if covered with white fire. And beyond the first figure emerged a second, and then a third. A startled gasp swept the room. For a moment Estevan thought the devil must truly be in league with El Popé, and then he remembered Father Andres telling him about a mixture of sand and liquid that produced a glowing appearance in the dark. If not a devil, El Popé was at least a magician!

El Popé, his eyes closed, his hands still outstretched, ceased his chanting. Without turning, he asked, "Who are you and why do you come to Taos Kiva?"

"I am Ca-ud-i and I bring with me Ti-lin-i and Tleu-me." The voice was deep and sepulchral and Estevan felt prickles move up and down his spine.

"We are spirits from the dead," the voice went on, "on our way to Lake Capala, where Satan dwells. We have been sent to earth to tell you that the time has come to kill the Spaniard."

And as the figure ceased speaking, the apparitions began to fade, growing gradually dimmer and dimmer until only the shadow of El Popé flickered once more against the kiva walls.

"You have heard!" El Popé's voice thundered once more through the silence. "Even Satan himself tells us that we must kill!"

The voice rose to a scream. "We must kill the Spaniard, kill! kill! kill!"

And a hundred voices took up the word. "Kill! Kill! Kill!"

"Kill! Kill!" Teri, across the room from his master, shouted hoarsely, "Kill! Kill!"

And Estevan, who understood the word, found his hands wet with sweat and his knees suddenly too weak to support him.

It seemed an interminable number of hours later that Estevan deemed it safe to attempt to escape the kiva.

After the meeting, there had been some ceremonial dancing and Estevan, his eyes smarting from the stifling, smoke-filled air, his head throbbing and the calves of his legs knotted from crouching, wondered, panic-stricken, if this was a dance that might go on for days. But it did not. It only seemed to, and at last every man had climbed the ladder and departed to one of the other Taos kivas to sleep. Thank heaven this was the great ceremonial kiva and apparently not used by the men for sleeping. Estevan would have been trapped for a certainty had that been the case. As it was, he thought, as he slowly inched his head above the opening in the center of the kiva's roof, things were desperate enough. He did not know what Jaime might have done. If Estevan were fortunate enough to escape the pueblo, would Jaime still be waiting at the arroyo? How many hours had it been since Estevan had come down into Taos?

It was with overwhelming relief that Estevan saw Jaime emerge from the shadow of the gully. Completely spent from his narrow escape and the steep climb up the slope, Estevan could say nothing except, "Thank God!" and sink panting upon the ground. But there was no time to rest. They must be well away from here before dawn and the sky was already showing a paleness beyond the mountains.

"There is—trouble," Estevan panted. "We must warn Governor Otérmin immediately!"

"What happened, Senor?" Already Jaime was tightening saddle girths and adjusting the stirrups.

"I'll tell you later. Right now we must ride!" And Estevan swung himself into the saddle and picked up Galante's reins.

Stopping only to rest and water their horses, the two boys rode as hard as they could toward Santa Fe. The terrible urgency of the need to warn Governor Otérmin spurred Estevan to greater effort than he had ever before made.

It was late the following afternoon when they clattered across the bridge and up the rise to the city. Across the plaza, reining in with a cloud of dust, Estevan leaped from Galante and dashed into the Casa Real. "The governor! I must see the governor!" he cried hoarsely to the guard at the door.

The soldier looked at the dirty, disheveled figure and, recognizing Estevan, said, "Just one moment, Senor, and I'll ask the governor."

"Ask the governor!" Estevan thought agitatedly. As if this were some trifle! Wait until Otérmin hears my news. There will be plenty of action then!

It was some minutes before the governor was free and could see Estevan. The young man, too excited to sit down, paced up and down the hall before Otérmin's door. When he was at last admitted, he wasted no time on amenities, forgetting his manners to such an extent that he did not wait for the governor to speak first but burst into a recital of the events he had witnessed at Taos.

When he had finished, Otérmin stood up and reached

over for the large earthen water carafe on the corner of his desk. Pouring a cup of water, he handed it to Estevan. "Sit down and drink this," he commanded.

Estevan did as he was told. "Now," said the governor sitting on an edge of his desk, "let me understand you clearly. You have just come from Taos?"

Estevan nodded.

"And you say El Popé was having a meeting?"

"Yes, Your Excellency."

Carefully, Otérmin questioned the boy. When he had finished, he sat drumming his fingertips on the desk top for a moment. Finally, he sighed. "Well," he said, "I appreciate your warning. Perhaps I should send a few soldiers north. But I suspect that El Popé is merely doing a great deal of talking to make himself big in the eyes of the Pueblos."

"If you had heard them, Your Excellency, you would not believe it was just talk. There was murder in their hearts!"

The governor grinned. "It may possibly be that, trapped in the kiva as you were, your evaluation was colored a bit. I am certain that had I been in your place, El Popé would have been equally terrifying. But can't you see how utterly impossible such a thing is? The Pueblos could no more unite in any action than England and Spain could. And El Popé has tasted the lash too often not to know the price of any such rash undertaking."

"But, sir—"

The governor stood up. "No," he said, putting his hand on Estevan's shoulder. "You have had a grim and dangerous experience but I am sure that the menace to the Spaniards is not as great as you fear. A few raids, perhaps, and forewarned, I shall take steps to prevent that. *Gracias*, my son.

Now go home and sleep for two days and the world will look safe once more."

Thus dismissed, Estevan turned and went toward the door, realizing suddenly how tired he was.

5

"This May Be Real Trouble"

As Governor Otérmin predicted, the menace of El Popé did not seem quite so imminent to Estevan after he had slept. Don Ramon agreed with the governor's appraisal of the situation. And Estevan, going the rounds of the hacienda and watching the patient, toiling Indians, found it hard to believe that anything could arouse them to the point of endangering the Spaniards. El Popé could rant and rave but any rebellion he might inspire would sputter out as soon as it met a show of force.

For a day or two, Estevan was haunted at unexpected times by the remembrance of his experience. The smell of piñon smoke might bring back disturbingly the chorus of "Kill, kill," but his feeling of unease was momentary as Estevan slipped back into the routine of the hacienda.

The weekend after his trip to Taos, Estevan looked up from checking Galante's hooves one morning to see the

Otéros, Juan and Felipe, cantering through the gate to the stable yard. They pulled up with a flourish, a thick cloud of dust rising from their horses' heels.

"Well, well, that nag of yours has gone lame already, I see," Juan remarked as he pulled off his riding gloves and tossed the reins of his horse to the younger Felipe.

Estevan grinned. "Lame or whole, he would outrun your horse and you know it," he rejoined.

Juan patted Galante's nose. "I hate to admit it," he sighed, "but I'm afraid you're right. He's a beauty."

Juan Otéro was famous for his escapades and more than once, Senor Otéro had threatened darkly to send him off to the military school in Mexico City. But with all his wild foolishness, there was not a more generous or good-natured lad in Santa Fe.

"Felipe and I came out to see if you can come and spend the night with us. We are getting up some races for tomorrow afternoon and thought you could pay a visit and let Galante show us what he can do."

He added, as if an afterthought, "Isabella is planning a little fiesta with some of her silly, chattering friends and I told her we would attend."

Estevan felt a glow of pleasure at the prospect of such a visit. A holiday with the Otéros, a chance to race Galante, a party with Isabella—what more could he ask?

"Come in and I'll see if I can get permission to leave." Estevan gave Galante over to the care of a stable boy and motioned to another to take the reins of the Otéros' horses. "Rub them down and water them," he directed the latter.

Don Ramon readily gave his consent to the visit. Such house visits were common among the Spaniards in New

Mexico, with people staying overnight or for days or weeks at a time at each other's houses.

Estevan left the young men enjoying a cooling drink and restrained conversation with Doña Magdalena while he went to his room to change.

Calling Jaime Chavira, Estevan ordered him to pack his saddlebags with fresh clothing. In a few minutes it was done and Estevan was ready.

"Oh, wait, my dear," Doña Magdalena said, rising from her chair as Estevan came back into the room. "I have an errand I would have you do for me in Santa Fe."

"Of course, Mother," Estevan said politely, though impatient to be on his way.

"Excuse me, gentlemen. Have a good ride and remember me to your parents." Doña Magdalena nodded to the Otéros who both bowed in response. "Come, Estevan. I have something for you to deliver to Father Andres."

Estevan's mother preceded him to her apartment. There she opened a carved wooden chest that stood before the patio window. "I have finished a new robe for St. Francis," she said, holding up a small, exquisitely embroidered satin vestment made to fit the wooden figure of Santa Fe's patron saint.

"I thought our dear Santos looked a bit shabby in the Corpus Christi Procession. Will this not look nice upon him?"

"It is beautiful. The good saint will be much pleased," Estevan said as his mother wrapped the little garment in a clean piece of linen. He knelt for his mother's blessing.

"God go with you, my son," she said, touching the top of his head.

The boys rode toward the city at a leisurely pace because of the heat of the August sun. To push their horses too hard at this time of day could easily injure them. As they passed a third trail that branched eastward from their north-south route, Juan suggested that they should drop over to the Hacienda Romero and pick up Carlos, also. They stopped and then Juan shook his head. "No," he decided, "he's probably still angry with me for betting on Sanchez at the last race. It takes him awhile to cool off. He's hotheaded, even for a Spaniard."

"Who won?" Estevan asked.

"Sanchez—that was the worst of it. I picked up ten reales because Romero was the favorite."

Estevan laughed. "You didn't have confidence in his horse even when everyone else did. *Si*, that does make your crime a grave one."

The Otéros lived in town. Senor Otéro's health was not good and several years previously he had turned the Otéro lands over to the management of his oldest son, Alfonse, and he and the senora and younger children had moved to a spacious house down the street from the Governor's Palace. The move had made Senora Otéro extremely happy because it not only freed her from the tasks of running the hacienda establishment but it gave her a most convenient location and opportunity to become a leader in the society of Santa Fe. Hardly a day went by that the Otéro mansion did not echo to the sounds of some lively social gathering.

When the boys arrived this afternoon, preparations were already under way for Isabella's little fiesta. Extra lanterns were being put up in the patio, a servant was carefully sweeping the hard-packed ground, and small tables and stools were being added to the heavy benches and other furniture of this outdoor living room. Supervising it all with relish and the voice of authority was Senora Otéro. Life was gay for people like the Otéros. Large houses and many servants made entertaining a pleasure. There were blooded Arabian horses for riding and hunting, and luxuries in clothing and furnishings to be had from Spain via Mexico City and the long supply caravan which journeyed northward each year or two through the endless sun-fired deserts of the south.

Estevan was disappointed not to see Isabella but realized that it was still siesta time. Senora Otéro had insisted that he and Juan and Felipe go to the boys' bedroom and rest for an hour. And when Senora Otéro insisted on something, no one refused —not even Senor Otéro. So reluctantly, like children, the three young men trailed off to the bedroom and flung themselves across the beds. Estevan had never felt less like resting in his life.

For awhile, the boys talked in a desultory way and then at last they lay silent, dozing. Estevan could hear, drowsily, the noises of the senora and her assistants on the patio, and then finally those, too, ceased and the only sounds that were heard were occasional street noises. For a while Estevan slept and wakened, intermittently. Then suddenly, he found himself fully awake, listening to the sound of voices outside.

The house, built around a hollow square, had few windows in the outer walls that faced the street. But there was a small one in this room, high up and vine-covered, that looked out on a narrow little alleyway. Several people, Indians apparently, had gathered there and the low murmur of their voices had awakened Estevan. He listened but could catch no words until, quite clearly, he heard "Popé." A chill went through him, out of all proportion to the small sound of the name. The voices dwindled away as the people moved on but Estevan lived again that scene in the kiva and he had a sudden, cold fear that Governor Otérmin and his father were wrong. There *could* be serious trouble and it might even now be rushing toward them! Estevan's spasm of foreboding could not withstand the gaiety of Senorita Isabella's party that evening, however. When he awoke the next morning in the guest room, he lay lazily enjoying the luxury of staying in bed past the usual hour, reliving the pleasure of the party as he listened to the servants crossing the patio. They would no doubt be serving the cups of pre-breakfast chocolate to the household. He was correct in his guess because in a few moments, there was a discreet tap on his door. As he called out, the door opened to reveal a moccasined Indian bearing a cup of the steaming, rich liquid.

Estevan sat up in bed and took the chocolate thinking, as he drank it, how glad he was the Aztecs had introduced this delicacy to Cortez and his fellow conquistadores. Chocolate made life infinitely more pleasant.

The sun shone through the window and cast a pattern on the red tile floor that rivaled the intricacies of the Indian rugs. Estevan closed his eyes and thought again of the loveliness of Senorita Isabella. She fairly sparkled at her party last night and was as elusive as a moonbeam when he had tried to have a word with her in private. What a beauty she had become! Estevan sighed and wondered if he were falling in love. His musings ended suddenly as the door opened and Juan and Felipe came into the room.

"Here you are, still lying abed when the world outside is calling to you!" Juan exclaimed. "Are you not ashamed?"

"Personally, I hadn't heard a sound," Estevan replied,

setting his cup on a stand beside the bed. "And I liked it that way," he added pointedly as he slid down in the bed and pulled the covers up to his chin.

Juan strode forward and with one hand yanked the covers from Estevan's hand and flung them in a pile on the floor. "*Up*, you lazybones! There are things to be done before we run that toothless, spavined old nag of yours in any race!"

Estevan groaned as he got up. "The manners of this younger generation," he said plaintively. "What has happened to them?"

Felipe grinned as he handed Estevan his clothes. Felipe was sure that his brother, Juan, was the funniest, cleverest and bravest young man in all of New Mexico.

Juan stretched out on the bed as Estevan dressed. "You know, manners *have* changed," he mused. "I was taught that it was unmannerly for a young gentleman to try to lure a senorita away from her duenna, but one sees it attempted sometimes by the most exemplary of young men today."

Estevan reddened. "What do you mean?" he bluffed.

"What do I mean?" Juan's voice was far away, as if he were almost too comfortable to talk. "The boy asks what I mean!" He yawned.

The yawn was smothered suddenly as Estevan picked up one of the bed bolsters and dropped it over his friend's head, holding it down in spite of the violent flailing of arms and bellows of protest that ensued.

Felipe thoroughly enjoyed the tussle between his brother and Estevan, but when they had worn themselves out and sat red-faced, panting and disheveled, he remarked quietly that unless they stopped playing like children they would be late for breakfast. The prospect of being unpunctual at Senora Otéro's table was enough to settle both young men down to the business of making themselves presentable. Breakfast was a gay meal, with everyone reliving the pleasures of the previous evening. Isabella was wearing a white dress with crisp ruffles and she had a fresh rosebud pinned at her throat. Estevan decided that she was even more beautiful than she had appeared the night before. He caught himself beaming fatuously at her whenever he had the chance, and Felipe had to kick him in the shin to alert him to help himself from the tray of corncakes the servant was patiently holding out. What a fool I am! Estevan told himself furiously as he saw the amused glances of the family. Isabella will think me nothing but a great moon-faced calf if I don't get hold of myself. And from then on, he tried resolutely not to look at the beautiful senorita.

"Juan," Senor Otéro said, "before you go off today, I'd like you to take some papers to Governor Otérmin for me."

"*Si*, Father."

The errand only involved walking over to the next building. Felipe and Estevan decided to go along and Estevan took his package for Father Andres. "I'll deliver this and then come back and meet you at the Casa Real," he said.

The plaza was quiet as Estevan crossed it. Soldiers stood guard around the Casa but did not take their duties seriously, leaning against the wall behind them or chatting amiably with each other as they paused in their patrols. As always, there were a few Indians about, some displaying handicrafts that were for sale, blankets and beads and baskets made of reeds or yucca fibers, as they gazed at the world with stolid, expressionless faces. Although they seemed indifferent to every-thing around them, their inscrutable black eyes missed nothing.

By the time Estevan had climbed the hill to the Church of San Miguel, he was perspiring freely. Father Andres was out, the servant told him in answer to his knock. Estevan left the parcel and trudged back down the hill to the plaza. How cool and refreshing the hall of the Governor's Palace seemed after the glare of the hot sun outside. But Estevan found his friend, Juan, anything but cool. He was striding up and down the wide areaway in a fever of impatience.

"The governor is busy," he said, "and I don't know how long I'll have to wait."

Felipe, lounging upon one of the hard wooden benches against the wall, yawned. "You'd better relax, Juanito," he said. "Wearing out the floor will do no good."

"This isn't my idea of the way to spend a perfectly good morning," Juan said glumly.

"You have to deliver the papers to the governor per-sonally?" Estevan asked.

"*Sí.* Father was definite about that."

Juan sat down and Estevan followed suit. The bench was as hard as it looked. For a while, the boys gazed around at the cracked and dirty plaster walls and listened to the chattering of some Indian women who were on their knees at the far side of the inner courtyard. The women were grind-ing maize in their flat stone metates.

The Casa Real fell far short of its name. An old build-ing, the first one of size to be built in Santa Fe, it was in bad disrepair. Estevan had heard Governor Otérmin remark that if the viceroy in Mexico City could not be persuaded to give some money toward the repair of the palace, it bade fair to come tumbling down about the ears of some future governor. "Or even of mine," the governor had concluded.

As they waited in the cool, dingy hallway, the young men gradually became aware that something was going on. At first they heard only the low rumble of voices from Otérmin's office. Then the door opened to admit a soldier and they could see several Indians inside the room.

"The warning shouldn't be ignored!" a voice said shrilly before the heavy door closed after the soldier.

"That was Don Francisco de Xavier," Juan remarked. "I wonder what's going on."

In a very few moments the soldier came back out, barked an order to the man on duty at the front door, then strode off across the plaza. A little later the Indians came out of the governor's office. Tanos Indians they were, Estevan noted absently as he wondered if perhaps now, at last, Juan could see Otérmin and deliver his papers. At this rate there wouldn't be time for any races this afternoon.

The Indians left, moving swiftly off across the plaza and disappearing down a street beyond. Then, just as Juan rose, saying he was going to knock directly on the door, the soldier who had left returned, this time with several other men. In their midst were two Indians—this time, Tesuques.

Governor Otérmin himself opened the door to admit the officer and the Indians. Immediately after their admittance, a babble of voices broke out that continued until a bellow from Otérmin stopped it.

"Is something going on?" Juan asked one of the escort soldiers who was lounging about waiting for the officer and the Tesuques to come out again.

79

The soldier shrugged. "All I know is that we rushed out to seize the Tesuques as they entered Santa Fe," he said.

Another soldier yawned. "Probably some squabble between the Pueblos," he remarked.

The boys waited, growing more impatient with each passing minute. "This is a fool's business, sitting here wasting a perfectly good day on an errand any slave could have taken care of," Juan fumed.

Finally he rose. "We've waited long enough. It's almost midday. I'll go back and tell Father that I'll try again this evening. Let's go."

As the three of them stepped into the street outside a horseman came galloping across the plaza from the north side. He paid no heed to anything in his path as he spurred his foam-flecked horse forward, scattering Indians and Spaniards from his path impartially.

"Look," Estevan said as the soldier flung himself from his horse, "he's wounded!"

Blood dripped from a cut on the side of the man's face. One jacket sleeve was ripped to shreds and he limped as he went into the Casa. The soldier on duty stepped forward to stop the man's entrance and the injured soldier fairly screamed, "I must see the governor! It is life and death!"

The boys paused. "What, in the name of all the saints, is going on around here today?" Juan asked. "All of this business with the Indians and the soldiers and now this rider!"

"I don't know, but *something* certainly is," Estevan answered. "Let's wait and see if we can find out anything."

People began to gather. They noticed a wound on the horse's hip and speculated among themselves.

"Did you see the blood on the soldier's face?"

"*Si*, dripping all down his neck."

"That was Captain Padilla who rode north with Father Dominic this morning," a man said. "I saw them go—Father Dominic and two soldiers."

"*Si*, riding to Tesuque. It is the day for the Padre's visit," another said.

In a few moments Governor Otérmin came out. His face looked suddenly old and drawn. The little crowd of people fell silent.

"There has been an uprising at Tesuque," the governor said without preamble. "Father Dominic and his escort were set upon and only Captain Padilla escaped. If any of you people live outside the city, get your households and bring them all here until we find out how widespread the trouble is."

He noticed the boys standing at the edge of the crowd and beckoned to Estevan.

"Did you ride in from the hacienda this morning?" he asked.

Estevan shook his head, his throat suddenly constricted with fear. "No," he said. "I came in last night."

"Did you notice anything amiss?"

"No, sir—nothing."

"Well, get back to the hacienda and warn your family to come in at once. This may be real trouble, or it may not."

"My father will not want to leave the hacienda, sir." Don Ramon, his son knew, was no man to run for cover at the first sign of danger.

"Well, tell him it is an order!" Otérmin snapped. "We have captured two Tesuques with messages for Tanos from

81

El Popé. We may have a full-scale revolt on our hands! Popé's been building up to something for years and this may be the real thing."

He turned to go back into the palace, then paused. "Take word to the Romero rancho, also."

"Yes, sir." Estevan turned and started on the run back to the Otéro house to get Galante.

"I'll go with you," Juan said.

"No," Estevan flung back over his shoulder. "There is no need for you to endanger yourself."

But when he reached the Otéro stables and began frantically to saddle Galante, Juan was already there getting his own horse ready and shouting orders to the stable hands. He instructed Felipe to tell Senor Otéro where he was going and why.

"But there is no need," Estevan protested again as he struggled with the saddle girth.

"There *is* need," Juan said quietly. "You may have great need."

Estevan was too distracted to protest further and in a matter of minutes he was pounding along the road north, with Juan close behind. A cold fear clamped itself around Estevan's heart. He had left the hacienda twenty-four hours ago. Anything could have happened in that period of time!

The Hacienda Romero lay to the south of the Algadonez lands and was reached by a smaller trail which branched off from the main north-south one. Estevan hesitated, begrudging the time it would take to detour, so anxious was he to know the situation at home. Juan came up beside him.

"You go on," he said. "I will warn the Romeros."

Estevan nodded and turned Galante. Then he swung

back again. The governor had told him to warn the Romeros and there was no knowing what Juan would be riding into. Estevan could not let Juan risk his life doing Estevan's errand. "We'll go together," he shouted to Juan. "It may be safer this way."

Urging their horses to move much faster, the boys tore across the ground. The Romero hacienda lay at the head of a small canyon on the edge of the mountains. As they swiftly covered the trail through the canyon, the boys began to see smoke rising from behind the rock cliffs. Indians signaling, Estevan thought, and his heart pounded to keep pace with Galante's flying heels. But as they were forced by the trail to rein in and go more cautiously, Estevan took a longer look at the smoke and knew that it was too much to be a signal fire.

When they rounded the canyon wall and looked down on the Romero hacienda, the boys understood the smoke. The hacienda lay in smoldering ruins with only parts of the shattered adobe walls left standing to mark the outlines of the once gracious home. A pall of smoke lay heavy upon the valley and the silence was complete except for an occasional crackle as fire ate away at the fallen roof timbers.

"Holy Mother of God," Juan muttered as they spurred their horses ahead, forcing themselves to ignore the sickness which was rising in their throats, and forcing themselves to go down to that grim ruin. They both knew with horrible foreboding what they would find but they had to make sure.

The bodies of Senor Felipe Romero and his son, Carlos, lay sprawled in the courtyard before the house. One glance told Estevan and Juan that they were past help. "What of the women?" Juan asked.

Estevan did not reply but dismounted on trembling legs. The body of a serving woman, horribly mutilated, lay across the doorway. Beyond, in the shell of what had been the great central hall of the house, lay three more bodies, pinned now beneath the smoking roof beams. But Senora Romero and Carlos' two sisters had not felt the beams fall, for they had been dead by the knife before any fire was started.

Estevan crossed himself and turned away. The horror of what he saw was exceeded only by the awful mounting fear for his own family. Were his own mother and father lying with sightless eyes across their doorstep? He turned in terror and flung himself upon Galante. Spurring him cruelly, he wheeled and galloped off. Juan lingered a moment, then followed.

The smoke of the fire mingled with the dust from the horses' hooves, and as the riders disappeared around the canyon wall, a vulture circled slowly above the silent desolation of the Hacienda Romero.

6

Rebellion

Estevan did not go back to the main trail to go home but went cross country through the desert. Skirting rocks and clattering across dry arroyos, Galante plunged on until they reached the border of the Algadonez property. Estevan tried to think neither of what lay behind him nor ahead of him. He leaned over Galante's neck and prayed silently to the Holy Virgin to keep his family safe.

As he approached the outbuildings of the hacienda, with Juan close behind, Estevan saw with relief that at least the place had not been put to the torch—not yet. A small group of people came from the outbuildings, running and carrying things in their hands. The boys reined up when they reached them. They were household servants and stable hands.

"What is it?" Estevan demanded. "Have the Indians attacked? Or have you attacked?" he added, noting that these were all Indians. By the saints, if they had he would trample them under Galante's hooves!

"No, no, Senor Estevan!" Maria the cook exclaimed, wringing her hands. "No, we would not attack the senor's family. But the Taos sent word. They are coming and we will be killed if we stay!"

"If you stay and help fight, maybe we can drive the Taos back!"

"No, Senor, it is not the Taos alone, but Tesuque and Tanos and maybe many others!"

Estevan said no more but urged Galante forward, leaving the refugees to straggle away to the mountains. If the Indian rumor had all the tribes rebelling, it would be suicide to try to make a stand.

Estevan and Juan did not leave their horses at the stable but clattered into the patio with them. Flinging himself out of the saddle, Estevan dashed into the cool hall, shouting for his parents.

"Father, Mother, where are you?" He ran to his father's office and pushed open the door but the room was empty. Running out and along the corridor, he came to their sleeping rooms. Not bothering to knock, Estevan burst open the door and paused in astonishment to see his mother rising to a sitting position in her bed.

"Sir, I remind you that no gentleman ever opens the door of a lady's room unbidden!" Senora Magdalena snapped at her son, her eyes sparkling with anger. "To disturb my siesta at all is discourteous enough, but to do so with such impropriety is unthinkable! Now, get out at once!"

For an instant, Estevan had a wild, hysterical desire to

laugh. Coming from the horrors of the Romero rancho to find his own parents placidly taking their usual midday siesta was almost too much for him. But the urgency of the situation steadied him. "Thank God, you are still alive!" he said.

He went to the connecting door. "Father," he bellowed, "arise at once!

"Mother," he said, turning again to the astonished, angry figure in the bed, "rise and dress immediately. We must flee the hacienda!"

"Estevan, have you taken leave of your senses?" his mother sputtered. "To address your parents so! And why should we leave? Leave to go where? Have you been too long in the sun?"

Ignoring the angry protests, Estevan went into his father's room. "The Indians have revolted!" he said. "The Romero family have all been murdered. Governor Otérmin says to get into Santa Fe as soon as possible!"

Don Ramon was already pulling on his jacket and fumbling for his boots. "Call Manuel," he said, "and Iago. We must have the servants pack."

Estevan said nothing but ran out to locate Manuel. He doubted that there were many servants left to do any packing or that there was time to worry about saving anything but their lives. "See if you can find anyone about!" he shouted to Juan in the patio.

The only servant they could find was Jaime. Juan located Manuel in his cottage. Going back to his parents, Estevan found his mother waiting for her maid, Estellita, to come and help her dress.

"Mother, for the love of God, get yourself dressed!

Don't you realize that we may be set upon and murdered at any moment!" Estevan exploded. "Estellita has fled, as has almost everyone else."

"All right, if I may have some privacy I shall do my best," the senora replied with dignity. She waited until Estevan had gone back to his father before she moved. Then, sighing over the unhappy state of affairs, she arose and dressed.

Frantically, Jaime, Manuel, Juan and Estevan worked to harness horses to a couple of carretas. Both Don Ramon and Doña Magdalena insisted that they must take some of their possessions with them into Santa Fe. "For how can we stay there without even a change of clothing?" Doña Magdalena protested when Estevan demurred about taking time to pack anything.

"You are overly upset, my son," Don Ramon said calmly. "The Indians may have attacked a few places, but they are too capricious to launch any real rebellion. I strongly suspect that it is unnecessary even for us to go into Santa Fe. By nightfall the marauding parties will have faded back to the pueblos, and the servants will have returned."

Estevan, remembering vividly the horror at the Romero hacienda, could not share his father's viewpoint.

"Jaime," Estevan ordered, hoisting a small trunk into a cart, "go up to the roof and see if you can see anything."

Jaime put the bundle he was carrying into the cart and sprinted across the stable yard and up the ladder that stood at the corner of the house. Climbing to the roof, he shaded his eyes against the blinding glare of the August sun and gazed around. Nothing—there was nothing but desert and mountain and sky. Not that we would see them if they were around, he thought, knowing how an Indian could melt into the landscape and become an invisible part of it when he chose.

He watched a "dust devil" whirl across the sandy waste to the east. They were common enough phenomena, little whirlwinds of sand lifting and dipping and dancing across the desert. But as he watched, Jaime was struck by the fact that this dust devil was not behaving normally. It was moving rather slowly and instead of lifting and swirling along above-ground, this was clinging to the surface of the desert. And suddenly, Jaime knew what it was.

"Indians!" he shouted. "Indians to the east!" He scrambled down the ladder.

"How many?" Don Ramon, carrying his strongbox, paused.

"Not a very large party, but they must be on horses, judging from the dust!"

"It could be soldiers," Don Ramon suggested. The idea of a group of Indians on horseback seemed too unreal to accept.

"Father, for the love of heaven, don't take any chances!" Estevan implored. "We must get away before they come. Five of us will only make a good target if it is Indians!"

"Be still!" Don Ramon ordered sternly. "Is it possible that my son is a coward who would run at the first sign of danger? This land was not won by cowards, and it will not be held by cowards!"

Doña Magdalena came out of the house and across the patio to the stable yard. She was carrying the two great silver candlesticks she had brought with her many years before, when she had come as a bride from Spain. "Jaime," she said, "bring a cloth from the chest in the hall. These must be wrapped so that they will not get scratched."

Estevan began to feel that he was caught up in one of those nightmares where one tries to lift one's feet and finds it impossible to move. Silver candlesticks and talk of cowardice when sure death was riding toward them across the desert!

"Senor Manuel," Don Ramon began, turning toward the overseer who had been saddling the riding horses. But Senor Manuel was no longer there and as Don Ramon raised his voice to call him the sound of horses' hooves fading in the distance broke the stillness.

"Well," Estevan said grimly, "that leaves *four* of us to defend my mother and the hacienda!"

Don Ramon seemed a little shaken. "Yes, perhaps we had better not take a chance. Jaime, take one cart—Estevan, you ride the other."

From a distance, echoing across the rolling desert, cries and yells and the beat of horses' hooves reached the stable yard. Estevan ran over to the ladder and climbed up to look out. The riders, Indians, could be distinguished now, their scarlet and blue and orange blankets flying as they clumsily rode their unaccustomed mounts.

Estevan clambered down the ladder. "Father, it *is* Indians and they will be here in minutes. Our only chance is to mount and ride. There is no time for wagons. I'll take Mother with me on Galante. He can carry us both. Juan, *make* Father *come!*"

Without waiting for a reply, Estevan ran out and leaped on Galante, then rode over to the cart where Doña Magdalena was struggling to pack the candlesticks securely.

Without a word, Estevan reached down and scooped up his mother's slight figure, settling her in front of him in the saddle. The sounds of the approaching Indians grew louder.

"Are you coming, Father?" he shouted, excitedly wheeling Galante and ignoring the shrieking protests of Doña Magdalena.

"Si!" Don Ramon at last realized the desperateness of the situation and he and Jaime mounted their horses swiftly. As Juan leaped into his saddle and the four horses plunged across the stable yard and out to the trail, the Indian raiding party was just approaching the outbuildings of the ranch. There were screams and derisive yells and an arrow whizzed by Galante's head as the fleeing Spaniards urged their horses on faster.

Estevan prayed that the inexperience of the Indians on the horses they were riding would slow them down. And, please, God, let their mounts be tired.

For a few desperate minutes the Indians gave chase and the distance between the refugees and their pursuers became dangerously close. But gradually the Spaniards picked up speed and the Indians dropped behind. Estevan wondered why there were no more arrows, then realized that the Indians were too busy managing their horses to be able to do any shooting.

At last, all of the Indians except one left the chase. The sole pursuer followed until the Spaniards topped a rise and gained additional speed as they headed into the valley below. At the rise, the Indian checked his horse and watched the four riders descend the hill.

This time you are safe, the Indian thought grimly, but

only for a while, amigos—only for a while. And Teri sat proudly astride the horse that only this morning had belonged to Carlos Romero.

Santa Fe was almost unrecognizable when the Algadonez family reached it. The quiet little town had been transformed.

"Was it only this morning that we waited so impatiently to see the governor?" Juan asked as they drew in their reins and looked around.

Estevan shook his head. "It doesn't seem possible," he said.

The plaza was alive with people, horses, donkeys, chickens and dogs, all making noise in their own way until the sounds blended together and were scarcely distinguishable. The braying, barking, screaming and cackling had merged into one vast cacophony of noise which beat against the ears in pulsating waves.

Over in front of the Governor's Palace the noise and confusion were compounded. The refugees found a spot to dismount and Don Ramon assisted his wife from her uncomfortable seat in front of Estevan. Doña Magdalena had finally realized the magnitude of the danger they had just escaped. The trail from the north bore enough grisly evidence in the form of torn and mutilated corpses to pierce the complacency of any Spaniard who had survived. Men, women and children, refugees from the north, had been set upon and savagely killed, their partially clothed bodies, carrion for birds and beasts of the desert, left to rot in the sun.

Doña Magdalena had hidden her face in Estevan's jacket and he had felt her body shake with sobs. Now, dry-eyed and dignified, she took her husband's arm as they made their way through the crowd to the entrance of the Casa Real. Estevan tossed Galante's reins to Jaime and turned to follow his parents.

"You and your parents are most welcome to stay with us," Juan said to him.

Estevan looked up at his friend. "Thank you," he said wearily. "You are kind. And *gracias*, also, for going with me."

"It is nothing," Juan replied soberly. "I will come back as soon as I have seen my father." He turned his horse and walked him slowly through the crowd as Estevan went into the Governor's Palace.

Inside the Casa Real, things were in even greater turmoil than outside. The Casa was of the usual Spanish-style architecture: a huge hollow square with the numerous rooms of the structure enclosing a large, open courtyard or patio. The central hall of the palace opened on the patio, as did many of the other rooms, and Estevan could see that already many refugees were taking up residence in the open air. Outside, as in the hall and corridors, people were huddled together, many with their faces blank and stunned, mute testimony to the horrors they had witnessed.

The governor's door opened to the Algadonez family, and Otérmin left a group of officials, who were engaged in a violent discussion of the situation, to come and speak to them.

He bent over the Doña's hand. "Thank God you escaped," he said. "Messengers tell me few did from the north."

He turned to Estevan. "Did you reach the Romeros?"

Estevan shook his head. "They were dead when I arrived," he replied, his voice flat.

The governor's face looked even more grim. "God rest their souls," he said, crossing himself.

But there was no time to mourn the dead. "Were you able to bring anything with you?" he asked Don Ramon.

The ranchero shook his head.

"Any weapons?"

Don Ramon started to shake his head again but checked himself. "Yes, our guns are fastened to the saddles."

"Any ammunition?"

"No."

Otérmin sighed. "Our problem will be supplies if we are in for a long siege," he said.

"Senora, we can lodge you and your family in one of the palace rooms, but I fear others may have to share it."

Doña Magdalena inclined her head graciously. "We thank you for your hospitality," she said formally.

"Juan Otéro offered us a place at his father's house," Estevan told the governor.

"The Otéros will be here themselves before another dawn," the governor said grimly. "There have already been raids on the outskirts of the city.

"Father Francisco is in charge of all supplies," he went on. "He will procure what you need. Every man is expected to share in the defense. If you will excuse us, Doña Magdalena, I'll have someone show you to a room and ask that Senor Ramon and Estevan stay to help me."

For the next two days, refugees straggled into Santa Fe from the nearby countryside. As their stories were heard, Governor Otérmin gradually came to the conclusion that not only Santa Fe was in trouble but that the settlements of Taos and Sandia and Jemez and Santo Domingo and Isleta and all of the others, which he had believed could take care of themselves, might well be in mortal danger also.

By August twelfth, three days after the strike at Tesuque, Otérmin decided to send word to the people of every settlement in New Mexico to abandon their homes and head either for Santa Fe or for the protection of Lieutenant Governor Garcia's forces at Isleta, thirty leagues to the south.

Otérmin also sent a messenger to Lieutenant Governor Garcia to send reinforcements to Santa Fe, for it now looked as though the capital of New Mexico was due for a prolonged and bloody siege. He got the entire Spanish population of Santa Fe, as well as the two hundred refugees from nearby haciendas, within the Casa Real. Most of the people lodged in the courtyard, but every room of the Casa was filled to overflowing, also. The governor even gave up his own personal apartments to house a half-dozen families.

Each group of refugees that straggled in added details to the horrifying situation in which the Spaniards found themselves. Everyone killed at Pojuaque, four escaped at Santa Clara, all but two out of seventy killed at Taos, none left in Picuris, all killed in Gallisteo Valley. Each report was a tolling of the dead and each survivor began to wonder if this were the end of the world.

"This is no small local rebellion," Governor Otérmin admitted at last. "El Popé has aroused every last devilish pueblo to revolt."

"If you had let me kill El Popé as I had wished—" snarled Don de Xavier. The alcalde mayor looked pinched and waspish and his leathery face had a gray cast to it. He had not slept well for a week.

Otérmin turned on him wrathfully. "The if's of history

would fill volumes!" he snapped, "and we have no time here to lay blame. If we survive this holocaust, you are free to submit a report of my shortcomings to the viceroy!"

"Gentlemen," Don Ramon said placatingly, "we are fighting the Indians for our lives. Let us not fight each other, too."

Governor Otérmin flung himself into a chair. Those frijoles he had had for lunch were wreaking havoc with his digestion. He passed a weary hand over his eyes and tried to think. *If* the messenger had gotten through to Garcia, and *if* Garcia had survived, and *if* he could spare troops—Holy Mother of God, what a list of "if's"—they should arrive in another week. Surely, the Casa could hold out until then.

He looked around at the men gathered there. They were good men, all of them. Don Ignacio Sanchez and his son, the alcalde mayor, Don Ramon Algadonez and Estevan, Don Diego Otéro with two stalwart sons, Lieutenant Isidero Chavez. With men of courage like these, they could outlast any Indian attacks.

"Father Francisco, have we adequate supplies for a siege?" the governor asked.

"*Si*—though I fear for water if the Indians should seize the Little Santa Fe," the priest answered.

"Yes, all they have to do is stop the flow into our acequia and we are desperate," the governor said. "Have every available container filled for emergency. Lieutenant Chavez, will you see to that?"

"*Si*, your excellency."

"That should spoil the Indians' plans if they tamper with the Santa Fe," Estevan remarked the next day as he and Lieutenant Chavez counted the water reserves.

"They probably know right now how many buckets we have on hand," the lieutenant replied. "For I misdoubt there is anything going on outside *or* in the Casa that the Indians don't know about."

"You think they are just biding their time?" Estevan asked.

The lieutenant shrugged. "Who knows what goes on in the mind of an Indian?" he asked. "They could be leaving us alone to make us overconfident. They probably figure that we can't possibly store enough water ahead to last any length of time. They will shut it off when they are ready."

As the lieutenant went off down the crowded corridor, stepping over dogs and children and bundles of personal belongings, Estevan looked after him and wondered soberly what would happen to the women and children when there was no water. He gazed up at the sunlight as it shimmered on the patio and suddenly its brilliant, dehydrating rays seemed menacing. Dear God, he thought, even the sunshine is a threat!

"You look as if you carry alone the burdens of our defense," a voice said at his elbow.

Estevan glanced around to find the Senorita Isabella. Despite a wrinkled gown, she looked her usual lovely self, her eyes sparkling and her dark hair glossy under the thin scarf which covered it.

"Well," Estevan said modestly, "it isn't generally known, but Governor Otérmin *has* put me in complete charge."

"How wonderful! That means the Indians are already defeated even though they don't know it," Isabella exclaimed with mock admiration in her voice.

"*Sí,* they have no chance at all against my natural cunning and military ability."

"One almost feels sorry for the Indians." Isabella moved out into the courtyard, her slender figure straight and graceful as she walked. The thought of Carlos Romero's sisters crossed Estevan's mind and the lightness of his banter with the girl was suddenly flat in his ears. Did the fate of the Romeros also await Senorita Isabella and the rest of them? No, that could not be! God would not desert his people for the savages. All they needed was faith and courage, and victory would be theirs!

Estevan straightened his shoulders. Courage and faith had won Nueva Mexico for the Spaniards in the beginning and they would hold it for them now.

Juan and Felipe Otéro and Ignacio Sanchez came wandering by as Estevan was trying to decide what to do until his turn at guard duty came along. Inactivity was one of the worst problems the refugees faced. Everyone was so tightly packed in with everyone else and nerves were stretched so taut that there was no relaxation or recreation possible for anyone except the hordes of young children who romped gaily about, getting into everyone's way.

The three young men greeted Estevan morosely as they sauntered out to the patio.

"Are you just off duty?" Estevan asked.

The Otéros nodded.

"I'm not on until the third watch," Ignacio said.

"Personally, I'm beginning to wish the Indians would attack just to give us something to do," Juan said, yawning. "You know what I'd like?" he asked, stepping across a fat, brown baby that had crawled, unattended, across the paving stones in front of him.

"No, what?" Estevan asked.

"I'd like to go for a swim in the river."

"An excellent idea," Estevan agreed sarcastically. "Would you prefer the Little Santa Fe or the Rio Grande?"

Juan considered. "I'll settle for the Little Santa Fe," he decided. "There's a pretty good hole right under the bridge and enough water there to get wet all over."

Suddenly, he stopped. "And why not?" he demanded of the others. "Why not a swim?"

"Do you like bathing in your own blood?" Estevan asked mildly. "That is what it would amount to by the time a few of the Tesuques got to you."

"Not if they don't see me!" Juan said dramatically.

"And how would you manage that?"

Juan beamed as if waiting for the question. "How about a swim in the moonlight?"

"Are you serious?" Estevan demanded.

"Of course."

"Then you're crazy." Estevan started to turn away. There were plenty of opportunities to die these days without going out and looking for them.

Juan grasped Estevan's arm. "You mean you're afraid?" he asked. He was smiling but there was just the faintest hint of contempt in his voice.

Estevan pulled his arm away. "I'm not afraid to die," he said, "but I flatter myself that I'll be more useful to Governor Otérmin alive than dead."

"He speaks sense," Ignacio agreed. "Our duty is to give our lives in battle, not waste them in a child's prank."

But to Juan Otéro, opposition was only a challenge. He turned to his younger brother. "Felipe, surely you aren't the noble coward that Estevan and Ignacio have become?"

Felipe, who sought every opportunity to win the admiration of Juan, shook his head vigorously. "No, I'll go along with you whenever—"

The rest of his words dwindled away as he saw the anger in Estevan's face.

"Just watch whom you call a coward!" Estevan snarled. "I'm no more a coward than you are!"

"All right, then prove it!" Juan insisted.

For a moment the two young men glared at each other. Then slowly, Estevan relaxed and grinned. "All right," he said. "By the saints, I'll show you!"

At midnight, a reluctant Estevan found himself carefully picking his way through the crowded patio to the small door at the rear of the Casa Real, waiting for his friends to appear. He shivered in the cool night air and thought glumly that a swim at midnight was far less appealing than at midday.

There was a little sound at his shoulder and Estevan looked around to see the Otéros approaching through the shadows. There was only Ignacio to wait for now.

"Maybe Ignacio isn't coming," Felipe whispered to Juan.

"He'll come," Juan said confidently. And he was right, for Ignacio soon joined them. What Spanish gentleman dared refuse to prove his courage?

"We'll slip out of the door one at a time," Juan said, working quietly to slide back the heavy beam that barricaded it.

"But that will leave the door unsecured while we are out," Estevan protested.

"It won't even be noticed," Juan said, dismissing that small consideration airily as he edged the door open.

"The Indians may be watching."

"You know as well as I do that they don't do any fighting at night."

Estevan's stomach churned with anxiety. If he backed out now, he knew that his peers would consider him a coward.

Juan slipped out into the blackness. Taking a deep breath, Estevan waited a moment and then followed him. Outside, the sky seemed only a pale gray and the moonlight, alarmingly bright. Estevan ducked low and scurried to the shelter of scrub mesquite which grew on the slope. He waited a moment, feeling as though he were the target for a thousand arrows. Then he moved cautiously along the curve of the hill toward the stream. Beyond the Little Santa Fe and up the opposite rise, Estevan could see the smoldering campfires of the Indians. But there was no visible movement of the enemy and he began to think that maybe he and his friends would be able to see this mad escapade through without mishap after all, incredible as that would be.

Slipping along silently, the four boys managed to reach the riverbank. A feeling of excitement gripped them as they began to undo the laces that fastened their clothes. When they had slipped off their clothing, they eased themselves quietly into the river, making little grunting sounds as the icy water touched their bodies.

In the excitement and darkness, Estevan snarled the laces of his trousers. Try as he would, he could not get the knot untangled. The others would be all through with their swim before he could even get his clothes off, he thought frantically. He gave a wrench, trying to break the cord, but to no avail.

Concentrating as he was on the laces, Estevan was not aware of the Indian standing on the riverbank until he heard a shrill war cry. He looked up in time to see his three friends leap from the river with one accord, then scramble for their lives up the riverbank and head for the Casa, their naked bodies gleaming white in the moonlight as they made their escape. Then, surprisingly, Estevan heard laughter. The Indian was chuckling as he watched the spectacle.

Estevan held his breath and shrank back in the shadow of the bridge. The Indian's sense of humor might be tickled by the sight of three naked Spaniards in full flight, but it would not apply to another Spaniard lurking ten feet from him. Estevan's mouth was dry with fear and his heart pounded loudly as he crouched, watching the Indian.

The man was joined by a couple of others as he stood there. He explained the joke and they, too, appreciated it. Would they decide to search for any other Spaniards, or would they assume that was all of them? Desperately, Estevan looked around for a weapon. He had left his *daga* at the fort and now he could not even see a stone nearby that he might use.

But the three men did not do any searching. They turned and strolled back up the hill. For a long time after they were gone, Estevan sat in absolute stillness, fearing almost to lick his dry lips. When he began to feel that the Indians were truly gone, his mind tried to cope with the problem of getting back up the hill and into the Casa Real. And the more he considered the problem, the more impossible it became.

The Indians were sure to be keeping a closer watch now and if he were to try to get back to the Casa by going up the hill, he would inevitably be seen. And even were he to make it safely to the Casa, he would surely be seen and attacked before he could attract attention and convince the guard that it was truly he who sought admittance.

Estevan moved to ease his cramped muscles and tried to still the panic that had risen within him. He must think. He could not let fear master him. Could he get in by the main gate if he made his way around through the town? The outer buildings of Santa Fe would give him some cover if he went down the river a bit, and once he got into the city he could approach to within a few feet of the Casa Real without crossing any large open spaces. But, there again, could he get admitted before an Indian arrow found his back?

Estevan looked at the waning moon and knew that there was one thing which he had to do. He had to get away from this spot under the bridge before dawn, when the Indians on the hill would be coming down to get water. Again, he fought a growing panic. He could not leave and he dared not stay. What was he to do?

7

The Choice of the Cross

The night grew blacker and a coyote howled his serenade to the moon. Indian dogs took up the noise and repeated it in a rising chorus. Estevan shuddered. Familiar as such howls were, they held a menace this night. It was the thought of the Indian dogs that roused him to action. He would take a chance on the town. All it would take was one whiff of a white man's scent to bring the whole pack—dogs and Indians both—down upon him.

He reached down, unlaced his shoes and tied them around his neck. Then, crouching and picking his way carefully and quietly, he began to creep along the edge of the river in the lee of the bank. The water was icy cold against his ankles, and his teeth chattered uncontrollably.

Fiercely, Estevan clamped his jaws together and inched his way along the river, expecting each moment to hear a shout of discovery. But the Indians were so sure of their victims bottled up in the Casa Real that they were not keeping too careful a watch. Did they not hold the city, the valley—indeed, the whole of New Mexico? They awaited only an order from El Popé to attack the Casa Real and finish the matter completely.

Estevan was unnoticed and unchallenged as he carefully made his way downstream to where some buildings straggled unevenly between the town and the river. Reaching a point opposite the nearest building and crouching even lower than before, he moved slowly across the little stream and up the bank, then slid gratefully into the deep blue shadow of an adobe hut.

Sitting down on the ground, Estevan rubbed his feet, now chilled and numb, and put on his shoes. He had devised a plan and, with the help of God, had a chance to regain the safety of the Casa when dawn came.

The sky began to show pink behind the Sangres as Estevan skulked in the shadows of the tavern across the plaza from the Casa Real. There were not many Indians in Santa Fe, even though they could roam it freely, and Estevan hoped that he could attract the attention of the sentry atop the Casa Real and then make a dash for the door of the refuge and have it opened to him before an Indian arrow found him. It was a desperate gamble but the only way.

Suddenly Estevan tensed, every nerve alert. There was the sound of voices as a group of men came along the street. Deep in conversation, they were walking slowly. At the corner of the tavern, not four feet from Estevan, the men stopped completely. Taos, they were, and Estevan listened intently, trying with his scanty knowledge of Taos dialect to understand the argument.

Why wait, one was protesting. "We should attack at once and kill them."

"But not until El Popé gives the signal," another said. "He is the leader."

"Then why doesn't he give the signal?" the first demanded. "If we wait too long, there may be help from other Spaniards!"

"What other Spaniards?" a third man asked drily. "The Spaniards of Taos or Tesuque or Santa Domingo or Ácoma?"

"There are forces at Isleta."

"Yes, but we captured the messengers who went from here and let Garcia think Santa Fe is already wiped out. Why would he send troops north when he believes it already too late?"

"I still say that we gain nothing by waiting. My people grow restless," the first one grumbled as they moved on.

For a moment, in his dismay at the news he had overheard, Estevan forgot his own immediate peril. There would be no help from Isleta! The refugees at the Casa Real must survive or perish by their own efforts.

The morning of August fourteenth dawned so hot that by an hour after sunup the stones in the courtyard were already warm to the most toughened feet. By midday, the very cactus would be drooping, Jaime Chavira thought as he stood his watch atop the Casa. Jaime shielded his eyes against the hot glare of the sun and looked out over the landscape. Not a breath of air stirred.

For a few moments, he gazed northward across the rolling hills that lay between Santa Fe and the Hacienda Algadonez and thought of Estevan. Why the senor had ever taken part in such a wild prank was a mystery. But these aristocrats were a mystery to him anyway. Doña Magdalena had sobbed over her lost silver candlesticks when candlesticks had ceased to matter at all, survival being the only important thing. Now, Senor Estevan had lost his life to prove his courage and the whole matter seemed silly and of little consequence —as silly as the wild-eyed, naked swimmers had looked when they dashed into the patio.

Not even the awesome name of Otéro had saved the boys from all kinds of gibes from the other refugees. Governor Otérmin had been so furious at the escapade that he had cut the boys' rations in half and doubled their duty. Well, it had been a break in the monotony at any rate, and no harm done, except to Senor Estevan, of course. Doña Magdalena would have something besides her silver candlesticks to cry about, when they told her.

Jaime turned his gaze southward, his eyes searching the landscape carefully. In that direction the land stretched away level except for a few mountains which rose sharply from the plain. Far away to the south, Jaime knew that the plain ended in a sudden escarpment, the land falling away sharply to a much lower level. That was the area of the Santo Domingo and San Felipe Indians. And far away to the south, beyond the escarpment, lay Isleta, the southernmost of the pueblos.

Jaime strained his eyes, wishing that he might be the one to shout the glad tidings of the arrival of Governor Garcia's forces from there. But no dust ruffled the surface of the desert, and no figures broke the brilliant pulsating blue of the New Mexico sky.

Reluctantly, Jaime narrowed his gaze to the town of Santa Fe spread out below him. The sinister quietness of the empty plaza sent a chill up his spine. How many of those surrounding blank walls sheltered Indians waiting for the signal to attack? And why had not the signal been given?

Jaime's attention was caught by a movement in the shadows of the tavern building across the plaza. He watched, his fingers tightening on the harquebus he held in his hands. He called to another on guard duty and pointed, asking, "Look, Raphael, what is that?"

The other man came closer to the edge of the roof but before he could speak, Jaime knew the answer. For the figure emerged momentarily from the shadow and, looking upward to the roof of the Casa Real, gestured to himself and to the Casa door. Jaime recognized Senor Estevan. By all the saints, it was like seeing the dead!

Jaime knew at once what Estevan was asking and he ran over to the inner edge of the roof and shouted to a guard to tell the governor that Senor Estevan was outside and would want admittance. Then Jaime went back to his post. Raising his harquebus to his shoulder, he scanned the area of the plaza to see if any Indian might be lurking where he could endanger Estevan.

But the plaza seemed completely deserted. It was not until Estevan emerged from the shadows and sprinted across the corner of the open park that a blanket-clad figure arose from behind the low wall of the alcalde mayor's house and raised a bow. Jaime saw him and as he pulled back the arrow, the harquebus roared and the man spun around and fell, his bow clattering against the wall. Several Indians came running out of the tavern and others from the streets that branched out from the plaza. Jaime and the other guards atop the Casa flung themselves to the roof to avoid the arrows which came soaring through the air.

The Choice of the Cross

As Estevan dashed toward the door of the Casa, he prayed that it would be opened quickly. For unless it was, his body would have a dozen arrows in it before he could knock a second time. As he pounded on the door, he heard the explosion of Jaime's gun. To Estevan, expecting each second the searing cut of arrows into his flesh, it seemed interminable until the heavy door swung grudgingly open, although it was actually only a moment until he was safely inside the fort.

There was a babble of excitement all around him as Estevan found himself clasped in Don Ramon's arms.

"Thank God. We thought you dead!" Don Ramon said huskily. Then he stood back and glared angrily. "And it is no fault of yours that you are not!" he added sharply. "That a son of mine could play the fool at a desperate time like this!"

"I know, Father, and I am ashamed," Estevan told him.

Don Ramon started to say something more, then considered the people standing around gaping and remembered his dignity. "I will speak with you further," he said as he turned away.

Estevan, flushed with embarrassment and his knees trembling with the excitement of his narrow escape, looked up to meet Governor Otérmin's stern gaze.

"Well," the governor said grimly, "I share your father's mixed feelings."

"*Sí,* your excellency," Estevan said humbly, "but, sir, would you speak with me privately?"

"You wish your punishment meted out without an audience?" the governor surmised.

"Yes, sir," Estevan lied. It would hardly do to spread

109

panic among the beleaguered refugees by telling them that their one real hope, relief from Isleta, was a vain one.

Behind the closed door of the governor's office, Estevan told his story of the Indians' conversation. Otérmin leaned back and rubbed his hand over his eyes and down his jaw, now rough with a stubble of beard.

"Well," he said at last, "that means we have no hope of help from any quarter." He rose and walked over to the shuttered window, lost in thought. When he turned back to Estevan, he seemed to have a new grip on himself.

"No help from any quarter—except the Lord," he amended, "eh, Estevan?"

"Yes, sir," Estevan agreed.

Otérmin seated himself again and gazed at Estevan. "And now, with death staring me in the face, I find myself having to mete out punishment for boyish pranks which befit a schoolroom rather than a beleaguered fort. What have you to say for yourself?"

"Nothing, sir. I am heartily ashamed," Estevan admitted.

"Good," the governor said briskly. "I'm glad you show that much good sense, at least. When one admits to having played the fool, he is on the way to learning something. I'll give you the same treatment I gave the others: double duty and half rations for a week. You, however, are escaping the tongue-lashing the others received. I find it hard to work myself up again to such heights of oratory as I displayed to your naked, shivering friends," he added drily.

"Thank you, sir," Estevan answered. "I—I believe, sir, that I can imagine what I missed."

The governor's eyes twinkled. "I was quite impressive," he said. Then he spoke briskly again, dismissing Estevan. "See Lieutenant Chavez about your duties and then get some rest," he directed.

Estevan had to endure a stern lecture from Don Ramon and the tearful remonstrances of Doña Magdalena before he was able at last to sink into troubled sleep in a corner of the room his parents shared with ten other people. It was the last sleep he would have for three days.

Estevan's watch began in the cold hours before dawn. Doña Magdalena insisted that he wrap an extra blanket about his shoulders as he made ready to leave. He did it to humor her, but was glad of the warmth as he stood atop the palace. The guard had been doubled because across the Little Santa Fe, Indian watch fires had leaped high all through the night and there had been much noise and the glimpse of lithe bodies flashing in silhouette around the crackling flames.

"Look sharp," Lieutenant Chavez warned as he made the rounds. "The Indians are building up to something, there's no doubt."

"Yes, sir." Estevan shouldered the heavy harquebus and turned his eyes toward the north where new fires glowed on the hill behind the church of San Miguel.

Jaime Chavira came on duty at the beginning of Estevan's second watch. When the two came together on their patrols, Estevan thanked Jaime for his help the day before.

"It was nothing, Senor Estevan," Jaime said.

"It was a great deal to me," Estevan insisted graciously, "and I hope someday to be able to give you proper reward."

"Thank you, Senor." Jaime moved off as he completed his area of patrol.

The sun had not been up twenty minutes before Estevan had to shed his extra wrap. He was considering doffing his jacket, also, when Jaime called. "Look, Senor, there is something happening behind the church!"

Estevan looked. A large group of Indians was forming and beyond, southward to the plains, a column could be seen approaching with the dust rising in the clear air like smoke from a campfire.

"Call the governor," Estevan ordered.

Jaime sprang to obey.

By the time Otérmin and Lieutenant Chavez had climbed to the roof of the Casa, the column of marching Indians was close enough to distinguish.

"Tanos," Otérmin said. "There will be action this day!"

As the column advanced, the group behind the church became larger and noisier and some of the men who were mounted rode out to meet the approaching Tanos.

Otérmin gave orders for every man to be alert, weapons ready, and stationed at all possible openings of the Casa. Women and children were herded into the patio, protected from random arrows behind improvised barricades of furniture and supplies. As the Indians approached, tension inside the Casa Real mounted.

This is it! Estevan thought. We are going to be attacked at last! And there was a sense of relief in the thought.

When the Tanos reached the southern edge of the city the troops broke apart and, with great screaming and shouting, began to plunder and pillage the buildings near them.

At the same time, the group at San Miguel began to ransack the buildings close to them, beginning with the church. The Indians emerged from their looting wearing parts of Spanish clothing, a fine embroidered coat, a sash tied around the head, a filmy mantilla floating from their shoulders. In many places, as they left a building, smoke began to puff and billow from windows and doorways.

The sun was fairly high above the Sangres when the two groups joined forces. As they came together, there was a great uproar and surging masses of Indians began converging on the plaza in front of the Governor's Palace. They gathered—a shouting, screaming mob, yelling insults and making violent gestures.

Estevan felt a little sickened at the manifestation of such intense hatred. After all the work of the good priests, after all the things the Spaniards had done for the Pueblos, it was incredible that they should feel so much hate.

Three Indians mounted on horses made their way slowly through the mob. One of them carried a sword and had on his head a tall, rakish, red satin hat. As the rider approached the Casa, Estevan recognized with a start that the hat was part of the outfit his mother had so carefully made for the Santo Francisco. A bitter feeling of anger swept through him at the sight of the insult to the good St. Francis.

When the three had reached an open place before the Governor's Palace, one held up his hand for recognition. The crowd of Indians fell silent.

The Indian spoke in perfect Spanish and the thought went through Estevan's mind that this man was a house servant, one who had been given special education by his master.

"I would speak with the governor," the Indian said. Governor Otérmin strode to the front of the palace roof. "I am here," he said gruffly. "Speak."

"I am war chief of the Tanos," the Indian declared arrogantly, "and I have an offer to make."

"Make it," Otérmin ordered.

The man fished around in the folds of his blanket and brought out two objects. Dramatically, he raised them aloft and the Spaniards could see that they were crosses: one white, one red.

"Behold, these crosses," the man said. "The Spaniard may choose whichever he desires. He may take the white cross and we will let him depart in peace from our land. Or he may choose the red one and we will fight him until no Spaniard lives in all of New Mexico!"

In the silence that followed his speech, the Indian continued to hold up the crosses. The scene was one of such absolute quiet that it looked like a painting.

This can't be real, Estevan thought. Who do those Pueblos think they are, that they can order the Spaniards out of the king's land?

Finally, Otérmin spoke and there seemed only an amused contempt in his voice. "I would hesitate to accept the white cross and have to trust my brothers, the Tanos, to keep their pledge of safety to me and my people," he said. "For I remember only a few days ago that my brothers, the Tanos, were on the side of the Spaniard and betraying their brother Tesuques."

He paused as an angry murmur arose from the crowd, then lifted his voice slightly. "The Tanos seem to change their allegiance as easily as our serpent brothers change their skins."

The Indian who held the crosses spoke again. "If the Spaniard is too weak to protect himself, he is better destroyed," he replied to the governor's taunt. "The Tanos do not intend to spill their blood for a people or a god who are made of shadow."

Governor Otérmin's hand gripped his harquebus so tightly that his knuckles whitened. "Neither the Spaniard nor his God is a thing of shadow!" he roared across the silent plaza. "Take your defiled crosses back to the heathen, Popé, and tell him we make no choice—we make no bargain with the Tanos coyote. We remain in the land of our fathers. We fight for our homes and our lives and, with the help of God, we will win!"

As the governor's words echoed through the clear air, a cheer went up from the men on the roof and from the people packed in the inner courtyard of the Casa Real.

The Indian spokesman threw the two crosses to the ground, turned and walked his horse back through the muttering crowd of Indians.

Otérmin turned to Lieutenant Chavez. "Order the cavalry to mount," he said, "and deploy more men on the roof. The time has come to fight. We'll make the battle ours by striking the first blow. We'll drive the skulking Tanos clear to El Paso del Norte!"

8
Attack

Before the Tanos knew what was happening, Governor Otérmin and his men were saddled up and sweeping out of the Casa Real to fall upon them with a violence born of these past days of outrage and frustration and pent-up horrors.

Because of the horses, Estevan, Juan, Felipe and the other young men were counted as cavalry. As they plunged out of the shelter of the Casa in the charge that marked the beginning of this first battle, Estevan's thought was a fierce exultation that here was action at last.

Most of the Indians had withdrawn from the plaza by the time the great double doors of the Casa Real spewed forth the angry Spaniards. Those who were still around fled at the sight of the rearing horses and to escape the sudden bark of the guns, from the Casa roof, that covered the cavalry charge.

But the Tanos did not flee very far. At the edge of town

they made a stand before the smoking ruins of San Miguel, and Estevan suddenly found himself in a hornets' nest of sword-wielding, knife-throwing, arrow-shooting Pueblos. For a moment he felt confused. Where did one start to fight? The problem was solved for him as he saw an Indian lift a sword to slash at Galante's forelegs. Estevan immediately pulled back on the reins, rearing Galante, and at the same time slashed out with his own sword.

There was a crunching, jarring impact as blade met bone. Estevan pulled his sword back and found another target in an Indian who had seized the back of his saddle and was attempting to pull him from his mount. From that moment, there was no time to think, to feel, or to plan. It was a fight for survival, and Estevan cut and thrust and parried, bringing into play all the knowledge and skill of sword fighting that he had learned from his father. Time ceased to have any meaning. There was only attack and counterattack, only the sight and smell of blood and the shouts and screams and battle cries of Spaniards and Indians.

Governor Otérmin seemed to be everywhere. Once, Estevan looked up to see him impale a Tanos on his sword, thrusting so hard that the hilt was against the Indian's chest. Juan Otéro was unhorsed but continued to fight, shouting the old Cortez battle cry, "St. Jago and at them!"

Slowly, imperceptibly, the Tanos retreated southward, the Spaniards pressing them back inexorably. But as the Indians retreated through the streets of Santa Fe one by one, the buildings billowed smoke, and flames all but obscured men from each other so that it was difficult to tell who was friend and who was enemy.

At length, Otérmin called a halt for his men and they rallied around him in the churchyard of San Miguel.

"They are on the run. Let us go after them!" Estevan cried.

In answer, Otérmin turned and pointed with his blood-stained sword to the hills north of town. There, silhouetted against the sky, were hundreds upon hundreds of Indians!

The days that followed were a continuing unrelieved nightmare for the hard-pressed people of Santa Fe.

The Indians to the north proved to be a combination of forces: Tiguas, Tehuas, Taos, Queres—and even Apaches. The sight of the latter brought home to Otérmin, with full impact, a realization of the extent of the revolt.

"How that devil, Popé, managed to unite the Apaches and Pueblos in a common cause, I'll never know," he told his council.

"Never in my lifetime have I known the Apaches and Pueblos to be friends," the alcalde mayor agreed. "Popé has planned well."

"With them united, resistance is useless," Senor Otéro said. "Can we not parley with them?"

"To what purpose?" Otérmin asked. "We have nothing to bargain with."

"The Indians have no stomach for siege," Lieutenant Chavez said. "If we can skirmish with them and take a high enough toll of life, they may tire of it and retreat." But even he did not believe his own words.

"*Si*," the governor sighed. "It is a faint hope but I see no other course. We have no chance, now, of retreat."

The weary hours dragged on. Three times the Spaniards emerged and fought, killing many but having to retreat each time to the Casa because of the overwhelming numbers of the enemy. Day and night the plaza was filled with shouting, screaming Indians dressed in Spanish clothing they had taken from the bodies of their victims.

Spanish losses in the skirmishing were slight but even the loss of one man was too much when there were so few. Governor Otérmin was wounded in the chest but, mercifully, the wound was not serious.

When he reached the safety of the Casa after one encounter, Estevan was astonished to find an arrow sticking through the shoulder of his doublet. He had no recollection of when it happened but it had missed his neck only by inches.

Three Indian prisoners were taken and questioned. They boasted of the number of allies who were rallying to the attack and told of the complete destruction at Isleta. When he had finished questioning them, Otérmin ordered the prisoners shot. They were taken to the roof, executed, and their bodies tumbled onto the heads of the Indians in the plaza.

Estevan, watching the execution, was sickened. He ran a trembling hand through his hair. Water, he thought numbly, I need a drink of water. Making his way down the ladder, he went to the patio where the conduit from the Little Santa Fe emptied into a cistern. A crowd of people stood around it. Pushing through, he tried to get to the gourds which served as common drinking cups. The gourds were there but when he reached into the cistern for water, he became aware of the talk around him.

"There is no water."

"What are we to do?"

There *is* water, he thought impatiently, a whole cistern full.

"There *is* water," he muttered thickly. "What are you people talking about?"

"Look, Senor."

It was Jaime Chavira, standing beside him. Jaime had been wounded in the arm when he went out as a foot soldier in the morning's fight and his bandage was red with blood.

Estevan shook his head to clear it. He had not slept for two nights and his mind was foggy. "Look at what?" he demanded.

Jaime pointed and suddenly Estevan's weariness left him as he realized what everyone meant. The conduit was dry. No water trickled into it. The Indians had cut it off.

"Go and tell the governor!" Estevan ordered Jaime. "We'll need a guard to save the water here." He set the gourd down.

"Get back," he ordered the refugees. "If our water is cut off, we'll have to ration all that is here."

A woman suddenly threw her shawl over her face and began to wail. Others took up the cry.

"Stop it!" Estevan ordered. "Stop this at once. We have water stored. We aren't without reserves. But we must use it carefully."

But the wailing continued. Children, not knowing why their mothers were crying, also cried, and the bedlam did not stop until the crowd parted when Governor Otérmin came striding across the patio.

Taking a look at the dry conduit, the governor turned to the people. "Don't be alarmed," he said. "We have plenty of reserve. With rationing, we can hold out for days. From now on, you will each be given your portion, morning and evening. No one is to use any water without permission. The Indians haven't defeated us with this any more than they have with their fighting."

The wailing subsided but others besides Estevan and the governor knew that this was the worst blow yet. As Estevan watched Otérmin make his way back to his office, an idea formed in his head. He followed the governor.

"Your Excellency," he called, "may I speak with you?"

"*Sí.*" Otérmin led the way to his office and closed the door behind them. "What is it?"

"Your Excellency, we don't know that the forces at Isleta are wiped out. Could we not make one more attempt to get through to them?"

The governor shook his head. "It is too remote a chance."

"But it *is* a chance," Estevan persisted, "and perhaps our only one. My horse can outrun any other in New Mexico. Let me try to get through to Isleta. If I can make it, I can bring help before the water is gone."

Otérmin considered, looking at the disheveled but eager young man before him. The lad had a level head—in spite of that fool escapade he took part in—and his mount was, in truth, a fine one. Perhaps he had the dash and daring to succeed in such a hazardous undertaking.

The silence in the room was broken by yells from Indians in the plaza.

"Two would have a much better chance than one," Otérmin said at last, slowly. "In case of attack, one might break through." He thought over the available ones that could go. It should be a younger man—one with the physical

stamina and raw courage necessary to face such a rash undertaking. The young Otéro? No, he was rash but he was also one
of Otérmin's best cavalry men and the governor could not spare
both him and Algadonez.

Estevan had an idea. "Let Jaime Chavira go with me.
He is a good horseman and has courage."

"Chavira?" Oh, yes, the Algadonez man, the governor
recollected. He did not know him, except as a servant.

"Think you he has the stomach for such an adventure?"

"Of course. He would do as I wished even if he didn't
want to," Estevan assured the governor confidently.

"Let me consult with Lieutenant Chavez. He knows
Chavira better than I. Come back in an hour," Otérmin said.

When the last blush of light had melted slowly from the
Sangre de Cristos and the Indians had settled down around
the campfires that surrounded Santa Fe and sentries were
beginning to think drowsily of their reliefs, two young men
quietly walked their horses through the postern gate of the
Casa Real and melted into the black shadows. Cloths
muffled their horses' hooves, and each bit of metal on the
harnesses had been wrapped so that there was no sound as
Estevan and Jaime skirted the base of the hill east of the Governor's Palace.

They did not mount and ride south but instead turned
eastward, taking a trail through the canyon that would carry
them along behind the Indians camped southeast of Santa
Fe. Once beyond them, Estevan and Jaime would only have
to avoid stragglers until they reached the Sandia Mountains.
But the Sandia Mountains would mean that Isleta was near
and if the Sandia Indians were hostile, it would not matter
much with the end of the journey so close.

As Estevan let Galante pick his way carefully over the rough trail, his thoughts were not so much concerned with the dangers of the trail as they were with the question of what the people of Santa Fe would do if there were no help from Isleta. Suppose the Indian reports were true and Garcia and his men had been wiped out? What then? Resolutely, Estevan pushed the thought from his mind.

High on the rim of a canyon, an Indian traveled swiftly along carrying messages to El Popé from the Sandias and Pecos in the south. The night sounds of the mountains were muted and it was as if the runner moved through a world empty of everything except himself and the soft night wind and moonlight.

Suddenly, the .quiet was shattered by the clatter of a rock tumbling down the hillside. It was not an uncommon occurrence. Sometimes a rock that had been imbedded for years would suddenly, for no apparent reason, loose itself and go crashing downward. The Indian runner paused and gazed for a moment over the canyon rim into the shadows below.

So quietly that they seemed to be wraiths, two riders slipped through a patch of moonlight that lay across the trail and vanished into the shadows of the canyon rim. The Indian watching knew that they were Spaniards.

When Estevan and Jaime left the dark silhouette of Santa Fe, with its danger of lurking Indians, behind them they urged their horses forward, making good time through the desert and low rolling hills east of the city. Reaching the mountains, they headed south and were forced to travel more slowly, letting their mounts pick their way along the rougher terrain. As they jogged quietly along, Estevan found it difficult to keep himself from thinking about the dreadful situation behind them. He had been painfully aware when he bade Doña Magdalena and Don Ramon good-bye that they might never see each other again. Doña Magdalena had clung to him and wept, and he had had to disengage her hands firmly.

"Don't cry, Mother," he had pleaded. "I'll return and bring help and in a month we'll be back at our hacienda and this will be only an unhappy memory."

That had distracted her. "Our hacienda!" she had sputtered. "A fine place that will be to return to! A heap of smoking ruins!"

"But think of the pleasure of designing a whole new house," Estevan had countered, easing away from her. "You can send to Madrid for all the fine things you've wanted, eh, Father?" Estevan grinned at Don Ramon.

"You had best mount and ride before you bankrupt me by putting extravagant ideas into your mother's head," Don Ramon answered gruffly as he put his arm around his wife's shoulder and drew her to him.

"God go with you, my son."

Thinking of all that depended upon his getting help quickly, Estevan felt a desire to force Galante forward at a faster pace. But good sense kept him from doing so. They were entering a narrow canyon and on both sides rock cliffs loomed, tall and black, against the dark sky. The trail ran close to the wall on their right, while to their left, a little below them, lay a riverbed. Dry now, it was a roaring, boiling, dangerous channel in the spring when snow melted on the tops of the mountains and sent water flashing into the lowlands. When Galante's hooves dislodged some loose

stones on the trail, they clattered down the rise into the riverbed, their sound shattering the stillness of the night.

The two riders moved on silently through the moon-
dappled canyon. A few more miles and they could make
their way westward out of the mountains and begin streaking across the plateaus that lay along the base of the Sandias.
When dawn came, they would seek a hiding place and rest
their horses for a few hours, then take their chances traveling
in daylight. They could outrun anything they met. The
danger lay in a surprise attack.

The trail turned, and ahead of them Estevan could see
the end of the canyon. Perhaps they could travel a little faster
now. . . . What was that shadow that appeared for a moment
on the rock where the trail turned? Estevan strained his eyes
but could see nothing. Had that been a shadow or was his
mind playing tricks on him? He slowed his horse.

"What is it, Senor?" Jaime came up beside him on the
trail.

"I thought I saw something on that rock ahead," Estevan replied, pointing.

Jaime searched the canyon with his eyes. "I see nothing,
Senor. But there could be an Indian in every shadow," he
added. His arm wound, though minor, ached and he wanted
to move on.

"It's best to take no chances. You scout the trail. If there
is anything, sing out and I'll make a dash to get through,"
Estevan ordered.

"*Sí*, Senor." Jaime dismounted and gave Estevan the
reins of his horse. It did not occur to either of them to debate
the question of who should scout and, if necessary, provide
a distraction to enable the other to get away.

Jaime melted into the shadows at the base of the canyon

cliff and edged forward, straining his eyes to see. A small clump of juniper grew beside the outcropping of rock ahead. As Jaime reached it, he was startled by a small rustling noise and looked down to see a snake slither away into the crevasses of the rock. Lucky for him it hadn't been a rattler, he thought. He crouched and looked around for any sign of life or movement. There was none. The only sounds were the sleepy twittering of the canyon swallows and the soft snuffle of the horses breathing as they and Estevan waited behind him.

There was no sound as an arm reached out from behind the juniper bushes and a well-aimed blow to the head dropped Jaime to the ground, as inert as a sack of grain. Swiftly, the Indian bound Jaime's arms behind him. Then he sat back and waited. One Spanish coyote in his snare, he thought. Patience, and there would be another. And when he, Taranche, went on to Taos it would be on horseback and with two prisoners to brag about! He squatted on his haunches behind the bushes, waiting.

Instead of spurring his horse forward, Estevan had dismounted and moved ahead cautiously to see what was keeping Jaime. The young fool, Taranche thought contemptuously. And these Spaniards had thought they could enslave the Pueblos!

Estevan came closer. Just a bit farther and Taranche could reach him. Clutching the rock firmly, he lifted his hand. There was a blow, the slight thud of a falling body, and Taranche had his two prisoners—and his two horses.

As Estevan began to regain consciousness, he thought that he was being tortured by the Indians. His head was splitting, bursting with pain. His arms felt stretched beyond human endurance, while across his stomach was such a weight that his internal organs seemed to be flattened as thin as a metate stone. And with this was a continual thudding and jolting that compounded his agony.

I must not cry out, he thought hazily. No matter what they do to me, I must not give them that pleasure. Then, as his mind cleared, he realized that he was not being tortured but that he was tied over the back of a horse and that Jaime was tied beside him. He lifted his head. "Jaime," he said, "are you all right?"

Jaime turned his head and grunted, "*Si.* What happened?"

"I was a fool," Estevan said painfully, between jounces. "I walked into a trap."

Jaime said nothing. The hours wore on and the boys had to clench their teeth together to keep from screaming as each jolt sent pain streaking through their bodies. From time to time, they lapsed into unconsciousness and when Taranche stopped at last to make camp briefly, both of his prisoners were insensible.

The Indian untied their hands and feet and let them fall to the ground. He then retied their wrists behind their backs. When Estevan came to again, he was lying on the ground and a tiny campfire nearby was sending its blades of flame straight upward into the silent sky.

Jaime, too, had regained consciousness now. He stirred and groaned slightly and the Indian came out of the shadows toward them. Speaking to them in the Taos dialect, he asked, "Water?"

Estevan nodded.

Taranche went away and then returned with a gourd full of water. He propped his prisoners against a boulder and gave them each a long drink. Then he pulled some maize cakes out of a small pouch slung over his shoulder and offered some to them. Again, the boys nodded and he fed it to them, shoving it into their mouths without any concern for their chewing capacity. Then, pushing them over on their sides again, he checked their wrist bonds and for good measure tied their ankles securely together. Satisfied finally that his prisoners could not escape, he withdrew to the other side of the fire and lay down.

When Taranche reached Taos with his prisoners late the following day, they were more dead than alive. Their bruised and pain-wracked bodies had dazed their senses so that they were only dimly aware of their ignominious entry into the pueblo, tied as they were like a stack of pelts across the horse's back.

They were tumbled off the horse amid a rapidly gathering crowd of Indians. As they lay helpless on the ground, they received a number of hard kicks, and children and women spat on them and pelted them with refuse. Finally, Taranche intervened and together with another young man hauled them off to one of the small pueblo rooms, shoving them inside.

For a while, the blessed relief of quiet after the rough jolting of the recent interminable hours seemed such exquisite comfort that Estevan lay dazed and unthinking. Then, as the pain subsided, his mind cleared and he began to comprehend the desperate situation he and Jaime had blundered into. With this realization came the unbearably bitter knowledge that not only were his and Jaime's lives forfeit due to his stupidity, but the lives of all those at Santa Fe, who were depending upon his getting through to Isleta, as well. He tried to think. It was night now, and they had traveled all day. There were twenty-four hours lost, and he was north of Santa Fe by a day's journey. This meant that he was three days from Isleta, even if he could escape. He groaned in anguish as he realized the extent of his failure.

"You are awake, Senor?" Jaime's voice came to him from the darkness.

"*Sí*," Estevan said. "Are you all right?"

"I am all right. Did you see—are we at Taos?"

"*Sí*, it is Taos."

"There is no chance now of our getting through to Isleta?"

"No, Jaime, there is none."

The finality of his admission of defeat to Jaime struck Estevan like the hand of death and he said no more. Even if escape were possible, he had no desire for it. Better to die than live with the memory of his failure. If only he had not been such a fool! If he and Jaime had spurred their horses and gone on past that rock. To be captured like rabbits in a trap by one unmounted Indian!

The noises of the pueblo community gradually quieted down and at last, everyone retired. Even Jaime's breathing came regularly now as he, too, found relief in sleep. But Estevan, his anguish of mind keeping him from the blessed comfort of unconsciousness, lay awake the whole night.

When the morning sounds of pueblo activity began— the crying of children, barking of dogs, an occasional shout— Jaime spoke. "Did you rest, Senor?"

"No," Estevan said.

"That is too bad. We will need all of our strength today."

"Yes. Pray God they will be brief with us." Estevan tried not to think of the horrors they faced before death would release them.

"I cannot seem to pray," Jaime said wistfully. "I have tried, but the words do not come."

Estevan was struck anew with his responsibility for Jaime's plight. A good master watched out for his servants. "Perhaps the Holy Virgin doesn't need our words, Jaime," he said gently. "Surely She can look into our hearts and know our need."

"I wish I had been a better person," Jaime remarked.

"*Si.*" It had never occurred to Estevan before to think about whether he was a good person or not. He had been Estevan Raphael Isidiro y Algadonez, and that had been sufficient. Now he wondered if that were enough. Was he good enough to win the intervention of the Holy Mother?

"Jaime," he said, "I am responsible for all of this, for your being here and for our capture. I am truly sorry. But I wouldn't blame you if you die hating me."

"I shall not die hating anyone, Senor," Jaime said slowly. "And least of all, you. You have always been kind to me. And as for our being here—we would be as bad off in Santa Fe. We face death at Indian hands wherever we are."

"You might still have had a chance if you were at Santa Fe," Estevan persisted.

"*Si*, but I would rather die this way, attempting to bring help, than by just waiting for the final storming of the Governor's Palace."

"*Gracias*, Jaime. That helps," Estevan said. He leaned his head against the wall. "Do you remember the time you were caught in your own jackrabbit snare?" he asked.

"*Sí*," Jaime said, smiling. "And you had ridden ahead and didn't know what happened. And I died a thousand deaths there on the desert, wondering if you would come back that way."

"And you never wanted to set a snare again."

"No—I knew too well how the poor creatures felt," Jaime admitted.

The boys talked, comforted by each other's presence, pushing back the dreadful thoughts of what lay ahead of them. Presently, there was a noise outside the tiny cell and the door opened. The two boys were dragged out into the open, the bright sunlight in the plaza blinding their eyes after the darkness of their prison.

They were hauled and shoved, and not given time to gain their footing, until finally they found themselves facing a large group of Pueblo men. Here it is, Estevan thought. Here is the end. Holy Virgin, give me strength! He stood up proud and straight before his enemies, hiding the terrible fear that overwhelmed him. And Jaime, too, stood erect, facing the Indians squarely.

9

"Pueblo Against Pueblo"

One man stood out among the Pueblos, towering above the others, his heavy braids as black as obsidian in the bright sun. El Popé.

El Popé looked at the two young men and a slow smile broke the stern pattern of his face, a smile that began and ended with his lips. His eyes did not change but retained their glittering black intensity, an intensity that showed no emotion, only an unfathomable hardness.

"So, we have two young senors to be our guests," El Popé said. "*Gracias*, Senors, for the fine mounts you have brought us."

Estevan ignored the sarcasm. He knew too well that argument or plea or threat were useless—that El Popé would enjoy nothing more than to draw him out in some way.

"Have you anything to say?" El Popé inquired with a mock courtesy.

132

Estevan remained silent.

Suddenly, in an action swifter than the eye could follow, El Popé uncoiled the rawhide whip he carried in his hand and it sang through the air, wrapping itself with searing pain around Estevan's neck. A scream of anguish escaped Estevan's lips before he could suppress it.

"Ah, that makes the young senor talk," El Popé exulted. "But that is only the first of your speeches, yours and your servant's," he added, his eyes flickering over the silent Jaime. "You will talk at our pleasure and dance to our music before another sun rises. And if you are fortunate, you will not live to see that sun."

He turned away contemptuously. "Tie the Spanish dogs to the poles," he ordered, nodding in the direction of some that were planted upright in the ground in the center of the plaza. "We will let the sun wilt them a little before evening."

"Wilt" was hardly the word, Estevan thought grimly as the sun climbed higher in the bright blue sky and its hot rays burned his unprotected face unmercifully. The cut from El Popé's whiplash smarted and throbbed as though it had been washed in vinegar. He wondered how long he could stand there without having his knees buckle, leaving him to sag against the pole like an animal carcass. He would stand straight and tall as long as he could, he determined. He ran his tongue over lips that were already dry and cracking and lifted his head to look at Jaime. Jaime was standing stiff-legged also, but his eyes were closed and his lips were moving as if in prayer.

Praying, Estevan thought. That is what I should be doing. St. Estevan—a prayer to St. Estevan might help. He concentrated on gathering his thoughts in prayer but before he had finished, a couple of little boys wandered over and began idly tossing pebbles and chunks of adobe at the two prisoners. However, it was too hot for the children to get much pleasure from their sport. Besides, so many Spaniards had hung from those poles recently that the novelty of tormenting them had worn off and the children soon drifted away.

Estevan, awakened from his lethargy by the interlude, looked around and noticed that the men of the pueblo seemed to be converging on the Great Kiva. A meeting to decide about him and Jaime? No, their fate had already been decided. Of that he was sure. It was probably plans for further attacks on Santa Fe. Dear Mother of God, how he had failed the people there. There was no hope—no hope at all. . . . His mind began to wander as the heat of the sun beat down upon his head. Imperceptibly, his body began to sag against the pole and he was not aware that the plaza was now completely empty except for a young man who was sitting in the shadow of the pueblo wall, cleaning a Spanish sword.

Teri was very much aware that it was his former master who hung there in the center of the plaza, however, and his thoughts were dreary as he worked on the sword that had come from Spain with the grandfather of Carlos Romero. How different the revolt was from what he had expected! There had been an excitement—a fierce, wild satisfaction—in those first few raids. The burning and plundering and killing had been a release for all the pent-up hostilities of the past. Revenge against the hated Spaniard had been sweet.

But then, when the blow fell at Taos itself and Teri watched Father Martinez humbled and humiliated before he was savagely butchered, he had felt a sickness. Father Marti-

nez had baptized him, and said words when Teri's parents
had died of fever two years ago and Teri had known him
only in kindness. There were those who said that the priest
grew rich from his levies upon the Indians and that he had
fine wines and rich foods, while the Pueblos starved. Perhaps that was true, but to see an old man forced to dance to
their gods—Teri shook his head and scoured his blade more
fiercely.

And now, the young senor tied to the post, to be butchered piece by piece this night. It was troubling, because
deep in his heart Teri acknowledged that he had known, as
with Father Martinez, only kindness at the senor's hands. In
spite of himself, Teri recalled the march from San Juan,
the near fight when Estevan intervened with the soldier, and
the blanket quietly put over the crying baby. Teri looked at the
drooping figure and felt sickness in his heart at the prospect
of this coming night.

Nicholas Bua, son-in-law of El Popé, emerged from the
kiva and walked slowly across the hard-packed, red-yellow
clay of the courtyard. His head bent, deep in thought, he
almost brushed against Teri before he saw him.

"You seem to be working hard on the Spanish blade,"
Nicholas said gravely.

Teri continued to polish for a moment before he replied,
"I polish because I like not my thoughts."

"Oh?" Nicholas Bua and his wife had taken Teri as their
foster son when Teri's family had died, and Nicholas was
part father and part elder brother to the orphan. He dropped
down beside Teri. "And what are your thoughts that they sit
so ill?"

Teri paused and gazed across at the Sacred Mountain.

"I—I suppose I am disappointed," he said vaguely, finding it hard to express his feelings. "The rebellion is not the glorious adventure I thought it would be."

"Bloodshed is seldom glorious," Nicholas said drily. "But I thought you hated the Spaniards enough to enjoy killing them."

"Yes, I did. I still do, except. . . ."

"Except what?" Nicholas prodded.

"Except that it is hard to see people like Father Martinez killed—and," he added, "him." He gestured toward Estevan.

"You no longer hate your Spanish master?" Nicholas asked.

"No," Teri said slowly. "I did because he was my master. Now that he isn't, I find myself regretting his death."

Nicholas did not reply and after a minute, Teri asked, thinking of El Popé's accusation, "Do you believe the priests make bad magic against us?"

Nicholas shook his head. "No," he said. "I cannot believe it of most of the padres I've known. They are not men to talk out of both sides of their mouths."

"Then why do we kill them?"

"Because El Popé says to." There was a note of bitterness in Bua's tone that caused Teri to look at him in surprise.

"The meeting in the kiva," Teri asked. "There was an argument?"

Nicholas stood up. "No argument," he said. "I cautioned against blood lust. Too many are killing for the pleasure of it, and El Popé rebuked me for weakness and Spaniard-loving."

He stood and looked at Teri's gleaming blade without seeing it. "I fear that in trying to rid ourselves of the Spaniard we have loosed a worse evil among us—the evil of violence. We invite the Apache and we kill without mercy and we may find that we cannot stop killing."

"You mean Apache against Pueblo?"

"Yes, and Pueblo against Pueblo," Nicholas said as he turned to climb the ladder to Taos' second story.

Pueblo against Pueblo, Teri thought. Never had he known of that. Pueblo against Apache, yes, but never against Pueblo.

Teri was still pondering the problem when Nicholas came down from the pueblo and walked out beyond the courtyard to the maize fields that were green and gold in the bright sunlight. His own fields at San Juan were being harvested by his wife and children, and he wished he were there overseeing them.

Teri watched Nicholas as he looked at the ears of corn, pulling back a husk here and there as if determining when it would be time for the women to start another picking and sensed that his friend found comfort in the familiar ritual of the fields.

Resuming his sword-polishing, Teri again found his gaze returning to Estevan's drooping figure. Freedom was what the Pueblos were fighting for. But why, Teri wondered, did freedom have to mean killing? Why couldn't Spaniard and Indian both live in New Mexico? Well, he told himself angrily, it has never worked that way before. Spaniards mean slavery. To end slavery, we must end the Spaniards! He tackled his sword now with such vigor that his rubbing threatened to wear the engraving itself off the hilt.

When a group of men came out of the kiva and toward him, Estevan lifted his heavy aching head. Had the time come?

No, the sun was still blazing high in the heavens—it was not evening yet. Oh, God, for a drink of water. His lips cracked when he tried to move them, and his tongue already seemed too large for his mouth.

The Pueblos did not heed Estevan or Jaime but strode purposefully past them across the sun-drenched courtyard and out toward the cornfield where Nicholas Bua stood. Estevan dropped his head forward again. Not yet.

Estevan's wandering mind was suddenly cleared by a shrill scream as Teri dropped his sword and ran across the plaza. "No!" Teri screamed. "No, you can't!"

Fully alert now, Estevan twisted his head to see what the trouble was. The men who had crossed the plaza were in the cornfield and they seemed to be throwing something at another Indian who stood a little beyond them.

Watching, Estevan realized that the Indian in the cornfield was being stoned. He stared, horrified, as the figure slumped to the ground under the merciless pelting from lava rocks. As Teri rushed past Estevan and flung himself, screaming, upon the executioners, Estevan, with a start, recognized him.

"What is it?" Jaime asked thickly.

"They are stoning a man to death," Estevan replied.

Teri's efforts to save Nicholas were no more effective than a fly buzzing around the Pueblos' heads. In less than two minutes Nicholas, his hands raised over his head in a vain attempt to protect himself from the blows, had crumpled to the ground. The Pueblos stepped closer, flung their last rocks and then turned, silent and stern, and walked away.

Teri ran over to the bleeding body of his friend, crouched

down and cradled the broken head on his knees. The movement brought a moment's consciousness to Nicholas and as his eyes opened, the smashed lips tried to form words. Teri bent closer to hear.

"Pueblo—against—Pueblo," the dying man murmured, and was gone.

Teri sat there, tears streaming down his cheeks, with the blazing sun and whispering corn a mockery of the peace which was no more.

As Estevan watched the forlorn figure, he wondered if the murdered man was the same one who had given Teri the headband that morning so long ago at San Juan Pueblo.

A tall man emerged from the kiva and walked with measured steps over to the cornfield. When a shadow fell across the body of Nicholas Bua, Teri looked up to see the lean, hard face of El Popé.

For a moment the leader gazed down at the crushed body of his son-in-law. There was no flicker of expression on his features. It was as if he were one of the carved *bulas* the Spaniards made of their saints. Santo Popé, Teri thought hysterically, Santo Popé had come to bless his son-in-law.

El Popé looked and knew that the weak counsel of Nicholas Bua would reach no more ears among the Pueblos. He turned away, content. And as the sun blazed at its zenith, Estevan's need for water became an agony so great that murder in a cornfield held little concern for him.

As the hours ground slowly by, the sun made its slow descent in the west. Sharp pains went through the length of Estevan's arms and then they became numb. He tried to turn and say something to Jaime, but his swollen tongue refused to obey. The sun seared his face and his shoulders burned beneath his shirt. As his mind wandered, he thought at times that he was dead and that the consuming heat enveloping his body was the fire of purgatory. In the blinding warmth of the August afternoon, all activity of the pueblo ceased, and even the dogs crawled into the shadows to sleep.

The sun's rays were forming long arms of slanting light, and a few of the women and children were stirring as a group of riders came into the plaza, rolling up a cloud of dust. They dismounted and shouted something at the nearby women. Estevan made a great effort to focus his pain-numbed mind on the newcomers. Apaches, he thought, but he could not think further. A boy, sent by one of the women into a kiva, came back presently with several men.

The Apache leader spoke rapidly, finishing with the word "Popé." The Pueblos nodded and then El Popé appeared, stalking across the plaza to were the newcomers waited. There was a conference and then El Popé barked orders. Other Pueblos gathered, bringing horses. In a few minutes El Popé and about twenty others mounted and rode off with the Apaches. Just as he wheeled to leave, he pointed to Estevan and Jaime and gave one final order before dashing away. Estevan thought he recognized the word "tomorrow" but he wasn't sure. He wasn't sure of anything, in fact, except the agony of his thirst and the pain which had enveloped his whole body.

When the dust had settled once more in Taos Plaza, a couple of men sauntered over and cut the bonds that held Estevan's and Jaime's arms above their heads, letting the two young men fall to the ground. A few kicks were an invitation to rise, but Estevan's arms and legs were so numb that he could not, and Jaime seemed to be completely unconscious.

One of the Pueblos said something. The other laughed and each one seized the legs of a prisoner and they began dragging them across the plaza to the pueblo building. At first, Estevan was acutely aware of the bumping his head was getting but by the time he was shoved into the little prison room, he was as unconscious as Jaime.

When he awoke later, faint and nauseous, he had no recollection of having been cut down. A noise at the door startled him into full consciousness. The door opened and a young man set a water jug and plate of food on the earthen floor. Estevan reached for the jug with trembling hands as the door closed again. He took a long draught, his unsteady hands spilling some down his chin. Then he said, "Jaime, Jaime—are you here?"

There was a slight movement nearby but no answer. Holding the precious water carefully, Estevan crawled across the floor, feeling ahead of him in the gloom for the body of his fellow prisoner. Finding him, he lifted Jaime's head and forced some water between the young man's teeth. Then he poured a little on his face. There was a stirring and his friend coughed weakly as the water trickled down his throat. "Here," Estevan said, holding the jug to Jaime's lips, "drink."

Jaime began to swallow eagerly, reaching up a hand to touch the earthenware jar.

"There," Estevan said finally, setting the jug down, "that is enough for now."

Jaime pulled himself upright. "What happened?" he asked.

"I don't know," Estevan said. "They brought us back to the cell. Can you eat?" he asked. "There is food."

"No," Jaime replied.

Estevan had no appetite either. He began rubbing his legs and arms, trying to stop the pain that still flickered through them.

Time passed and in the coolness of the room the boys, exhausted, slept. When they awakened, they were both refreshed and found that they were hungry. Estevan crawled back toward the door, located the food and went back to Jaime. After eating maize cakes and washing them down with water, they both felt much better. They wondered how long they had been there and why they were not being killed as they had expected.

"Maybe it is not time yet," Jaime suggested, and the thought was not a comforting one. They did not feel like talking and before they knew it, they had fallen asleep again. But it was an uneasy sleep of horrid, fearful dreams.

When Estevan awoke, it was with the feeling that something or someone else was in the room. He lay motionless, listening intently, his every sense alert. Was it an animal that filled the darkness with its presence? A snake slithering across the dirt floor? Was it better to call out, to frighten it, or should he lie completely quiet and let the creature— whatever it was—crawl away if it would?

Suddenly, a whisper broke the stillness.

"Senor," a voice said. "Awake, Senor, it is I, Teri." A hand touched Estevan's face. In spite of the warning whisper,

Estevan's nerves were stretched so taut that he almost yelped at the touch.

"Sh—" Teri said. "Make no noise. Arouse Jaime. Can you walk?"

"Yes," Estevan said, a thrill of hope surging through him.

"Good. You are leaving here."

Astonishment at receiving help from the recalcitrant Teri would come later. Right now, the hope of escape was the only thing that concerned Estevan. He crawled over to Jaime and wakened him. "We are being helped to escape," he whispered. "Come."

Teri had opened the door a crack, letting a shaft of moonlight slant into the little room. Jaime and Estevan made their way over to the hunched figure of their rescuer.

"Follow me. Keep in the shadows," Teri ordered. "I have horses saddled for you beyond the Great Kiva. Ride south. Don't go back to Santa Fe. Isleta still stands, but ride only at night until you get there."

"*Gracias*, Teri," Estevan said.

As silently as ghosts, the three figures emerged from the pueblo. Hugging the shadows, they skirted the edge of the building and then ran across the corner of the plaza to the Great Kiva, circling it swiftly to reach a huge outcropping of rock beyond. There stood two horses, saddled and bridled, and Estevan recognized with joy that one was Galante. He leaped into the saddle.

"Now, go quickly," Teri said.

Suddenly, without warning, a knife hissed through the moonlight and clattered against the rock, missing Estevan's head by inches. Then a harsh voice rang out and a figure leaped toward the boys from the shadows.

The attacker snarled Teri's name as he fell upon him. The two went down in a scuffle. For a moment they were a blur in the darkness as they rolled on the ground. The noise of the struggle aroused some of the dogs of Taos and they began to bark. There were sounds of people stirring. In a moment the whole of Taos Pueblo would be there!

"Go!" Teri shouted. "Go!" Breaking free for a moment, he crouched to meet the next attack of the other Indian. For a second, Estevan sat paralyzed in the face of this sudden development. Then his mind began to function. He wheeled Galante around and just as the Indian lunged at Teri, Estevan reached down from his saddle and, with unexpected strength, hauled the husky young man up onto Galante's back. Teri scrambled a leg astride as Galante plunged into the darkness beyond the pueblo, leaving Taos in an uproar.

They pounded along, with Jaime close behind Estevan and Teri. Estevan had no idea of the direction in which they were traveling. The important thing was to put distance between them and Taos.

"There is a narrow trail to the right, up ahead," Teri said. "Take it."

Estevan slowed Galante and, finding the trail, turned as directed.

"It is dangerous. Do not hurry," Teri warned.

The trail was indeed dangerous. It wound through the rocks and rose eventually into the mountains. The boys were forced to slow their horses to a walk. Estevan chafed at the snail's pace, listening all the time for the sound of hoofbeats behind them.

144

"Do not worry," Teri said, sensing Estevan's tension. "They will not expect us to be taking this trail. They will search to the south."

"Where are we going?" Estevan asked.

"To Blue Lake," Teri replied.

Estevan was startled. "Blue Lake? But that is—"

"Yes," Teri interrupted, "the Sacred Place. They will not think to look for us there."

Estevan rolled over and opened his eyes. Sunlight filtered through the branches of a giant pine and dappled his face. The air was filled with the fragrance of the woods about him and with another odor which reminded him that he was hungry. He sat up, trying to think where he was. The sight of Jaime and Teri at a small campfire brought back a clear recollection of the events of the past few days.

He looked around. Beyond the edge of the forest gleamed the unbelievably blue water of the Sacred Lake. Birds twittered and called and swooped in graceful arcs over the water, their bodies catching the glint of the early morning sun. Every muscle in Estevan's body ached, but he felt a sudden exhilaration as he realized that he and Jaime were free and, for the moment, safe. He looked at Teri, wondering why he had saved them.

Jaime looked around and saw Estevan sitting up. "You are awake, Senor," he observed. "There will be food in a little while."

"Good," Estevan said. He rose and stretched luxuriously, then walked over to where the horses were tethered. They were contentedly cropping at a patch of grass.

"You did well, my Galante," Estevan said, stroking the stallion's nose. Turning to the fire then and nodding toward the meat roasting on the spit, he asked, "What is it?"

"Jackrabbit," Jaime replied. "Teri snared it."

Estevan sat down beside Teri. "*Gracias* for your help," he said. "You saved our lives and at the risk of your own."

"I did not intend to risk my own," Teri replied sullenly.

"Why did you do anything?" Estevan asked. "Why didn't you let us die?"

Teri looked at him. "There has been too much killing," he said and turned brusquely away to tend the meat. But Estevan caught the pained expression in his eyes.

"The stoning yesterday," Estevan said gently, remembering the man in the cornfield, "it was a relative?"

"No, I have no relatives. He was my friend," Teri answered flatly.

"I am sorry," Estevan said.

"The meat is ready," Teri said, turning to Jaime and obviously wishing to change the subject.

Estevan, rebuffed, took the chunk of meat Jaime tore off for him and ate in silence. The boys were all ravenous and it seemed to Estevan that he had never tasted anything as good as this stringy jackrabbit.

When he had finished, Estevan rose and started for the shore of the lake to wash. Hesitating briefly, he asked Teri, "Is it all right if I wash in the lake?"

"Why not?" Teri replied curtly.

"I wondered—if it is sacred—"

"I have already betrayed my people and my gods by bringing you here. Wash if you will."

More mystified than ever at Teri's manner, Estevan walked down to the lake. Soon, Jaime joined him.

"How do you feel this morning?" Estevan asked.

"Better than I did yesterday," Jaime answered, grinning.
Estevan laughed. "And I, also," he agreed. Then he so-
bered. "Why did Teri do it when he hates me so?"

Jaime shrugged. "I do not know. For spite, to avenge
his friend's death, perhaps."

"His speech!" Estevan exclaimed suddenly. "He's speaking perfect Spanish, and when he lived with us he didn't
understand a word!"

"He spoke very fluently in the servants' quarters,"
Jaime replied, grinning again.

"Why, that wretch! I'll—" A flash of anger swept over
Estevan as he recalled his labored efforts to make Teri understand even the simplest orders.

"Senor," Jaime interrupted, "he is no longer your slave.
He is your savior now."

Estevan looked at Jaime and recognized the unpleasant
truth of his words. His anger died away and in its place was
a feeling of intense resentment that fate had placed him in
the difficult and awkward position of being obligated and
indebted to an Indian slave!

The situation was obviously no more to Teri's liking
than to Estevan's. The Indian boy had committed himself to
the Spaniards by his rash action and there was no turning back.
If the guard had not seen him, he would have sent the two
captives on their way, satisfied that he had had some small
measure of revenge against Popé. Also, that he had repaid
Estevan the debt he owed him for saving him from the mines.
But this—to be forced to flee from his own people—he had
not bargained for!

It was a strange trio camping there at Blue Lake for two days before heading south. Jaime, in the middle, could feel the antagonism and tension filling the air like heat lightning. Anything might trigger an explosion at any moment. Pray God they might reach Isleta without killing each other first, he thought anxiously.

10

Avalanche

The second night after the escape from Taos, Teri considered it safe enough to start south. "We will take the trail through the Sangres until we get to Pecos country," he decided. "Then we had better turn west to the Sandia Mountains or we may run into Apaches."

That sounded reasonable to Estevan. They would miss Santa Fe that way. He tried not to think about what might have happened at Santa Fe. Teri had said merely that it had fallen. Whether any had escaped or not, he did not know—or would not say.

When Teri and Jaime had the horses saddled and loaded with their meager supplies, Teri swung up behind Jaime. How times have changed, Estevan thought, when an Indian could mount a horse as casually as a Spaniard!

The first night's travel was uneventful. A mule deer

startled them by leaping across the trail in front of them but other than that, and the cry of night birds seeking prey, the boys seemed to have the world all to themselves. When dawn grayed the sky, they had covered a good many miles and were, Teri estimated, not far from Chimayo. They found a sheltered half-cave in the side of a canyon, where they could hide themselves and their mounts, and prepared to wait until nightfall before continuing.

Estevan chafed at the delay. "Couldn't we push on for another few hours?" he asked. "We are wasting a great deal of time."

"Indians are not like Spaniards," Teri said. "They rise early. This is the most dangerous time of all if we are to avoid them."

"Here is water, Senor," Jaime said, coming forward. "There is a tiny spring at the back of the cave." He handed Estevan a water pouch, cool and dripping.

"*Gracias*, Jaime." Estevan drank thirstily, then lay down on the sand while Teri and Jaime made preparations for the day.

"We had better post a watch," Teri said. "I will take the first half. Jaime, you take the second."

Estevan sat up. "I will stand my turn at watch, also," he said, angry at being ignored.

"Your pardon, Senor," Teri replied. "I had assumed the Senor was to be relieved of such matters as long as his servant and his slave were here."

The sarcasm in Teri's voice angered Estevan further and a bitter retort rose to his lips. But he clamped his teeth together and did not give voice to it. A quarrel would serve no useful purpose under the circumstances.

"I will take the first watch," he said shortly.

"Is that agreeable to you, Jaime?" Teri asked.

"*Sí*," Jaime yawned, "anything, as long as I can go to sleep."

Again, Estevan flushed with anger as Teri made it clear that no decision was up to him alone but subject to the wishes of the other two as well. The changed circumstances were humiliating to the young Spaniard. Had Teri saved his life, Estevan wondered, just to have such an opportunity as this? No, that did not account for his action, because he had not intended to flee with them. That had been forced upon him. Indians—Estevan thought with disgust as he watched the dawn approach in the distance. Could civilized man ever hope to understand them?

When Estevan awoke late in the afternoon, he found Teri gone and Jaime standing guard.

"Where is our friend?" he asked grumpily as he sat up, scratching an insect bite.

"He went to get food," Jaime replied.

"Good. I can use some. Where is that spring of yours?"

"At the back of the cave, Senor."

Estevan made his way back under the deep ledge. A small trickle of water dribbled over the stones into a shallow basin of rock. Estevan scooped some up in his hands and splashed it over his face. Refreshed, he went back to Jaime.

"I suppose he took one of the horses?" he asked.

"*Sí*, Senor."

"From now on, no Indian will walk when he can ride," Estevan observed bitterly.

"Do we Spaniards?" Jaime asked mildly.

Estevan looked at him sharply. "That is different and

you know it," he growled. "Or are you getting to be an Indian lover?"

"No, Senor. I only know that things will never be the same again in New Mexico."

"No, I suppose not," Estevan agreed gloomily.

Teri returned at dusk with a squirrel he had snared and a quantity of wizened yellow cholla cactus fruit.

"We will not overeat," he said, skinning the squirrel expertly, "but neither will we starve."

Jaime built a small fire in the lee of the cave wall and by the time darkness settled in, the boys had eaten their sparse meal and were ready to ride.

Estevan mounted Galante and then noticed a waterskin left beside the fire. Without thinking, he said, "Hand me the waterskin, Teri, and I'll fasten it to my saddle."

Teri, stamping out the fire, did not look up. "Get it yourself," he said. "I am no longer your slave."

The surly reply was too much for Estevan. He leaped from Galante's back, strode over and spun Teri around to face him, gripping his shirt. "You don't have to like me," he snapped, "but you *will* treat me with respect!"

Teri looked into Estevan's angry face and a wry grin curved his lips. "Respect!" he said. "That is the true Spanish conquistador. I give you your life and you demand respect."

"Don't forget that I gave you your life, too," Estevan rejoined. "Your own people would have carved you up in bits if I had not saved you back there at Taos!"

"Yes, and perhaps that is another reason for my hate," Teri said bitterly. "I have life, but only on Spanish terms, for among my own people I will always be a traitor."

Estevan looked at the lean young face before him, then loosed his grip and bent over to pick up the waterskin. It was true. Teri belonged to neither side now. Suddenly, Estevan felt unutterably weary. Life was filled with grim tragedy, he thought. Maybe the only fortunate ones were those who had already died.

That night was extremely cold for the boys. They had neither blankets nor extra coats with them and the temperature had dropped rapidly. Along with this, a slight drizzle had developed. As the night wore on the drizzle turned into a hard, pelting rain that soaked the boys and their horses and made the mountain trails extremely hazardous. They dared not stop, however, because their route lay along the Rio Pecos, and with the hard rain there was the danger of flash floods through the river canyon.

There was nothing to do but move slowly on and hope that the rain would let up. But it grew worse and along with it came thunder and great flashes of lightning which frightened the horses and made them difficult to manage. At one point, the mount carrying Teri and Jaime stumbled on the trail and went down on its knees, spilling the two riders into the mud. For a few moments the boys held their breath as Jaime checked the horse to see if it was injured.

"No, it seems to be all right," Jaime said at last, to their great relief.

But their difficulties were not over. The rain began to sting and in a few minutes the stinging became a hard pounding and bruising of hail. Stones the size of pebbles rained down until the horses, already overwrought and nervous, became almost impossible to manage.

"We'll take the next trail up the side of the canyon," Teri shouted above the clatter of the storm. "It will be dangerous but perhaps we can find shelter there."

Estevan's heart sank at the thought of guiding the restive horses up the side of the canyon but it was becoming too dangerous to stay here along the river bottom. Any second they might hear a roar and look behind them to see a solid wall of water rushing toward them.

Moments later, Teri and Jaime turned off and began climbing upward along a narrow outcropping ledge of rock. Estevan followed. As Galante picked his way along the slippery, rocky ledge, Estevan caught glimpses, during lightning flashes, of the sheer drop of the cliff and the snarling Rio Pecos farther below them. Pray God a sudden flash did not cause the horses to rear at this point! On second thought, that might be the easiest solution to their problems, Estevan told himself as he tried to pull his sodden shirt collar tighter against the pounding hail.

When it seemed as if they had been following the nerve-wracking trail for hours, the boys found, to their great relief, that it widened and the cliff wall became a sloping bank above and below them. They were out of the canyon now and on the side of a mountain where the slope was less precipitous, broken here and there by low-growing scrub oaks and piñons. The boys paused to rest the horses and themselves.

Jaime crossed himself as he gazed into the blackness of the treacherous route they had been following. "Thank the blessed saints for our safe journey through that," he said, relieved.

"I don't know that the holy saints would protect *me*,"

Teri remarked, "but somebody's gods are taking pity on us, for the hail is letting up."

It was true. The hail was turning into rain again and in a short time the hailstones, which lay as thick as snow on the trail and mountainside, would melt and the going would be less slippery and dangerous.

"We should be able to find shelter soon," Teri said as they began to move forward again. "That outcropping of rock up ahead—"

There was a sudden crack of lightning and a rolling clap of thunder and in the eerie white light Estevan heard a roar and looked up to see the whole mountainside moving toward them! Everything happened at once.

Estevan's shout of warning was lost in the roar of the avalanche and crashing of thunder and lightning. He pulled sharply on Galante's reins, rearing him back as the entire mountain, an avalanche of mud and stones and water, seemed to rush across the trail in front of him and downward to the river below.

There was the shrill scream of a horse and another flash of lightning. Then Estevan, trying to quiet Galante, had a glimpse of what had been the trail ahead. It was empty. Teri and Jaime had vanished, carried away by that tumbling, rolling, moving mountain!

For a moment Estevan stared, unbelieving, at the blankness before him. Then Galante reared again as the lightning continued to flash and Estevan had to concentrate all his attention on holding his seat and controlling the frightened horse. He backed Galante away from the flooded trail and sought shelter in a clump of pine, partway up the slope.

Dismounting, he flung the reins over a branch and went back to the spot where the flood was still moving sluggishly down the mountainside. As he stood there, looking helplessly into the black menacing avalanche with the rain pouring down and thunder rolling ominously in the distance, Estevan had never felt so alone in his life. His two companions just couldn't have been swept away in an instant like that!

As the lightning diminished, the mountain was in complete darkness. Estevan cupped his hands to his mouth and shouted into the rain-filled blackness, "Teri! Jaime!" Over and over he called their names, listening intently for some sound other than that of rain and wind and the gurgling of waters. But there was no reply. He looked around, frantic in his helplessness. There must be *something* he could do!

He dared not walk into the still-churning landslide. Although it was moving more slowly than at first, there was a terrific pressure which would sweep him off his feet and fling him into the bottom of the canyon. He had no rope to secure himself to a tree so he could investigate what lay below the trail in that void. But he *had* to get down there to find out if Jaime or Teri were alive. He could not wait for daybreak when at this very moment, they might be in desperate need of help.

Cautiously, he began to work his way down the mountain at the edge of the avalanche. Perhaps, if the lightning flashed again, he could get close enough to see something. As he sought footholds on the steep, treacherous slope, he was unmindful of the jagged rocks and knife-sharp spurs of scraggly bushes. Alternately sliding and stopping to call and peer into the blackness, Estevan was halfway down the mountain before there was another bright flash. But the light this time was too brief to help. It showed the roiling mud, stretching away in the distance, and some huge boulders and larger trees that were still standing. But more than that, he could not make out. "Teri!" he screamed again, "Jaime!"

Was that a moan he heard, or was it the wind? He listened, straining every nerve to hear. There it was again. It was a moan! "Where are you?" Estevan shouted, his heart leaping with hope.

"Here," came the faint reply.

Estevan plunged into the turgid mass of mud. He had to get through! But the rashness of his action was immediately apparent as his feet were sucked out from under him and he found himself rolling down the mountainside and swept with increasing speed toward the great rocks that edged the river!

Instinctively, he reached out to try to grasp at something to stop his descent. But his hands only scraped chunks of stone which, like him, were being drawn toward the flashing river. Then, as the rocks loomed ahead, large and menacing, Estevan's hands encountered a tree limb. It bent and gave with his weight but it held—and Estevan found his tumbling descent halted.

He clung desperately against the pull of the mud and was able to get a grip with his other hand, also. The branch was part of a good-sized scrub oak that seemed to be holding firm, and Estevan scrambled up to where he could hook one leg around a heavier limb. Panting with exertion, he rested a moment before he began to call again. But now, there was no reply. He had been swept too far from that weak voice to hear an answer even if there were one. For a moment the anguish of his disappointment made Estevan want to weep.

As a final flash of lightning from the diminishing storm cast its momentary brightness over the mountain, Estevan could see, less than ten feet below him, the body of one of his companions wedged between two boulders! Unhooking himself from his perch, Estevan slid down to the clump of rocks. As he reached the body he saw that it was Teri, and for one dreadful moment he thought he was dead. But a faint pulsation in Teri's chest told Estevan otherwise. He turned the inert form so that Teri's face was to the sky and began rubbing his forehead and wrists in an effort to revive him. After what seemed an endless interval, Teri moaned and tried to move.

"It's all right," Estevan reassured him. "You are caught in the rocks. Don't try to move."

Teri opened his eyes. "What happened?" he murmured.

"You were swept down the mountain by an avalanche," Estevan told him. "But you'll be all right."

"Jaime?" Teri asked.

"I don't know. I haven't found him yet. Are you hurt?"

"My leg—I can't move it."

One of Teri's legs was twisted under him in an unnatural position and when Estevan tried to move it, Teri winced with pain. Feeling it carefully, Estevan found that the shinbone was broken and protruding.

"Your leg is broken," Estevan said, looking around. If only he could see! He knew how to straighten the broken bones and bind them with splints but how could one find splints in a spot like this?

"If you can stand it until morning, I'll take care of it," he said. "But I must look for Jaime now. Don't try to move. I'll be back."

"All right," Teri answered, closing his eyes again.

The rain had ceased and brisk winds were pushing the storm clouds across the sky. As Estevan looked around, he saw that the moon had flooded the mountainside with its gentle glow and that the avalanche had nearly spent itself. The mud and stones were moving very slightly now. He crept from the shelter of the rocks and stepped cautiously into the sluggish mass, finding that footing, though still precarious, was possible.

He began making his way back up the slope, clawing for foot- and handholds. It seemed to him that for every step forward he slipped back two, but he kept going, refusing to accept the fact that finding Jaime in the dark on this broad expanse of mountainside was virtually impossible. Alternately crawling and pausing to shout Jaime's name, Estevan eventually reached what he thought was the place he had heard that first faint response. Off to his left, he could see a clump of mesquite or piñon that had held against the landslide. Perhaps Jaime had been caught in that.

When Estevan finally reached his goal he found to his bitter disappointment that the only things caught in the piñon were small scrub bushes and tree branches. There was no sign of his friend. He sank to his knees in utter despair as scudding clouds once again blocked the moon. An incredible weariness possessed him. What was the use of struggling, he thought. And then he remembered Teri, injured and helpless in the rocks below. He had to get back to him.

Prisoner of Taos

Starting back down the mountain, Estevan—confused in the dark—went beyond the piñon clump to his left instead of turning back the way he had come. In the darkness, he did not notice a deep fissure in the mountainside and before he realized it, he was tumbling headlong into the gully. Rolling helplessly, he could feel a resounding blow on his head. Moments later, his unconscious body landed in the mud at the bottom of the cleft.

Little diamonds of light sparkled before Estevan's eyes as he lay quietly. What were they? He had never seen stars dance about like that before. And he wondered numbly why he felt so cramped and cold. Had his blanket fallen from the bed? He reached down in the darkness, to pull it over him, and his hands encountered only mud and stones. The feel of the rough ground restored his consciousness and he opened his eyes and pulled himself up to a sitting position, remembering the sudden fall in the dark.

His head ached unbearably from the blow of his fall, but other than that, he seemed to be all right. His legs and arms moved, he discovered with relief, and he stood up. The sky began to show a paleness beyond the mountains. Thank the Blessed Virgin it was almost daybreak. He could go back and find Teri and take care of his leg. But Jaime—he had not found Jaime yet. With daylight, maybe he could. The saints willing, maybe even Jaime had survived this awful night. But perhaps Jaime had tumbled into the ravine, also!

Estevan called out, his voice startlingly loud in the still air of dawn. "Jaime, are you here? Jaime!" Over and over he called out as he worked his way along the bottom of the ravine. But it was no use. He could hear the noise of the river below and knew that the fissure would end abruptly in a sheer drop to the Rio Pecos a short way ahead. He had better start climbing the side to get back to Teri.

Faintly then, he heard a moan. He scrambled forward. "Jaime, is it you?" he called. Again, there was a moan, and then a whisper. "Here, Senor, I'm here," came the reply.

11

"You Called Me Estevan"

Exhausted from his night of terror and the almost impossible task of getting his injured companions back up the steep mountainside to the shelter of the pine clump where Galante waited, Estevan sank to his knees to rest. The sun was high in the sky and hot now, and Estevan realized that they were too close to the trail to be safe. Besides, Teri's leg had still not been attended to and there was a need for water. He could not rest yet.

He looked at Teri and at the ugly bone end sticking out. The skin was so taut that it seemed as if it would break through at any movement. He needed splints and something to bind them with. Estevan looked at the pine branches and then at the knife at Teri's waist. He bent over, taking the knife from the semiconscious figure, and cut a number of medium-sized branches. If they were trimmed and bound tightly, they would be firm enough. He took off his mud-smeared shirt and tore long strips from the bottom of it. Then he bent over Teri and, grasping his knee and the lower end of the broken shin-bone, gave a rapid pull, easing the bone end back into place. Teri jerked and gasped with pain. He was fully conscious now.

"I'm sorry," Estevan said, "but I had to straighten the bone. It will be all right now." Working swiftly, he bound the straight pine branches as tightly as he possibly could around the broken bone. It was a clumsy looking splint but it would serve the purpose.

"Rest and I'll see about food and water as soon as I've taken care of Jaime," Estevan said to Teri.

Jaime had no broken bones, as far as Estevan could tell, but he had cried out when Estevan picked him up to carry him. And during the grim struggle up the mountainside, he had fainted. But he was conscious now.

Estevan grinned down at him. "You look as if you'd managed to carry most of the avalanche on your clothes," he said.

Jaime tried to smile. "But not all, Senor," he whispered. "You brought some yourself."

"What we need is a woman to do our laundry," Estevan said, dropping down beside Jaime. "Can you tell me where you hurt?"

Jaime gestured toward his side. "There, with every breath," he said.

As Estevan carefully probed his side, Jaime winced. "You've broken some ribs, I suspect," Estevan said. "Here, let me have your shirt. There is no reason why you should have a tail to yours when I've already lost mine."

He tore as much as he could from the garment but there was not enough to bind around Jaime's chest. He did not dare tear up the whole shirt because they would need protection for their backs when they reached the desert. "I'm afraid it is not enough," he said.

"Take mine," Teri offered, behind them.

"*Gracias*," Estevan said, turning. "We'll all be tailless together."

"*Si.*" For the first time since they had known each other, Teri smiled at Estevan.

When he had bound Jaime's chest, Estevan took the knife and went off to see if he could find shelter and food and water. They could not travel for several days and they dared not stay in such an exposed place.

A couple of hours' search disclosed a cave in the rocks up above the clump of pines. There was no water close by, but Estevan could carry it from the river. The cave was deep and seemed uninhabited by anything more than a small whip-tailed lizard which slithered away at Estevan's approach. Estevan stood looking down the steep cliff he had climbed to reach the cave. There were enough good footholds to enable him to carry his companions up the cliff but it would be rough on them and virtually impossible to get Galante up there. They would have to tether the horse farther back among the pines and hope he would not be discovered. If he were, it would not take a very smart Indian to conclude that there were refugees nearby. Estevan could see no better solution to their problem, however.

Getting the boys up to the cave was a repetition of the earlier painful ascent of the mountain. But it was accomplished at last. Galante was fed, watered and hidden, the water pouches were filled, and Estevan had found enough juniper berries to satisfy the worst of their hunger pangs.

In spite of the pain of his leg, Teri seemed much better once they were settled. But Jaime's face was flushed and when he spoke, his voice had a high, thin ring to it.

"Jaime has a fever," Teri observed.

"Yes," Estevan said worriedly, "I know."

"You had better get some rest," Teri told him. "I can stay awake to give warning if there is need."

"*Gracias.*" Estevan stretched out on the ground, unutterably weary. "Don't let me sleep too long," he said. "If you or Jaime need something, call me."

Worn out from his twenty-four hours of exertion, Estevan sank immediately into heavy sleep and did not awaken until he felt Teri's hand on his shoulder the next morning. The sky was pink beyond the cave entrance, Estevan saw, as he sat up.

"You did not waken me," he said. "You let me sleep the whole night through!"

"You needed it," Teri answered. "But Jaime is worse and I fear he needs help."

Jaime's body was as hot to the touch as if he were in the middle of the noonday desert instead of a dank mountain cave. Estevan was frightened in his helplessness as he looked down at the restless, muttering figure.

"What can I do?" he asked. "I don't even have a blanket to put over him."

"Do you know the Hawimo plant?" Teri asked.

Estevan shook his head.

"It has a cluster of pale flowers and long, narrow leaves that grow up and down the stalk," Teri said. "It grows tall, usually in sunny places. If you can find one, bring as many leaves from it as you can. The Zunis use it for fever."

Estevan hunted up and down the mountainside until he found a clump of plants answering Teri's description. Galante whinnied softly, asking for attention, but Estevan merely patted his nose. "Later, friend," he said to the horse. "I will be back."

"Yes, that is the right plant," Teri said as Estevan handed him the leaves. "Now, lay them in the sun to dry."

When that was done, Estevan spoke to Teri about getting food. "There should be a mountain meadow up the trail. The slope grows less sharp beyond the landslide. Perhaps I can find some cholla fruit, and I'll set some snares for squirrels."

"Look for the jojoba bush. It has thin, pointed leaves and small fruits that look like nuts. Or get some century plant stalks—we can eat those," Teri said.

Estevan nodded. "I will return as soon as I can."

Estevan saddled Galante and watered him, then mounted the animal and walked him carefully up the trail that they had ridden the night before. He found that his guess had been correct. The slope grew less and less steep until it widened into a large meadow, lush and green with white and yellow and red flowers. Estevan drew in a lungful of the brisk, clean air and let Galante stretch his legs in a brief gallop. Then he dismounted and turned the horse loose to graze, while he looked for food.

He found several bushes bearing fruit, some of which he recognized and some of which were unfamiliar to him. He took off his shirt and gathered as much as he could into it, trusting Teri to sort the edible from the poisonous. Gathering some vines, he fashioned snares and set them carefully, saving a couple to put in the pine grove for squirrels. When he returned to the cave, he had a good-sized supply of fruit. Hopefully, there would be meat later, in the snares.

When Estevan entered the cave late that afternoon and put down his treasure, Teri looked at him quizzically.

"Why did you come back?" he asked. "I did not expect you to."

"What do you mean?" Estevan said.

"Why did you not go on southward and leave us? You could have made it easily to Isleta by yourself. With two of us injured, and only one horse, we'll never be able to make it."

"Yes, we will," Estevan said brusquely, angry that Teri had expected him to desert. "We'll all make it, or *none* of us will."

"I'll never understand the Spaniards," Teri said.

"Nor I the Indians," Estevan replied shortly.

The Hawimo leaves that Estevan had spread out on the ledge beyond the cave opening were dry enough now for Teri to crumble into tiny particles. He mixed these with water in one of the waterskins.

"Now," he directed, "rub this over Jaime's body."

Estevan did as he was directed, massaging the liquid into Jaime's burning skin.

The next two days were a nightmare for Estevan and Teri. Jaime grew violently delirious and at times it took both Teri and Estevan to restrain him from leaping up and rushing out of the cave where he would have dashed himself to death on the rocks below. All sense of time and concern for the future were forgotten in the immediate struggle to survive and take care of Jaime.

167

Finally, on the third day, the fever broke and Jaime began to perspire. By nightfall, when Estevan rubbed him once again with the Hawimo, Jaime's mind was clear. He asked for water and when given some, drank thirstily.

"*Gracias*, Senor," he murmured gratefully as he sank back against the pine boughs Estevan had cut for his bed.

"He's going to be all right!" Estevan said to Teri as he looked at Jaime's white face. "The fever is going."

"*Si*, Senor," Teri said, "you have saved him."

"Not I—*we*, Teri. Your Hawimo and your care as much as mine. And my name is Estevan."

Teri raised a quizzical eyebrow. "To an Indian, Senor? No, not to an Indian."

Estevan's temper flared. He wanted suddenly to shake Teri until his teeth rattled. "It is not the Spaniard alone who is arrogant and smug," he said sharply. "Look into your own heart. You will not accept my friendship when I offer it!"

For a moment, Teri looked at Estevan without answering. Then, shifting his damaged leg, he said, "You do not truly offer friendship, Senor Estevan. I have gratitude for what you have done for me and I respect you more than I have ever respected any Spaniard—except for the padres—but we can never truly be friends, you and I. When we reach your people at Isleta, you will see how it is. I will no longer be a human being in need of your help. I will be an Indian. And we will not eat at the same fire or sleep beside one another again."

Estevan turned away sadly, his anger suddenly gone. Teri was right, he knew. Among his own people, Estevan could not claim Teri as a friend and an equal. It would be too outrageous a thing in the face of his fellow Spaniards.

Once Jaime's fever had broken, his sturdy constitution asserted itself and he began to mend rapidly. Within a week he insisted that he was strong enough to travel. Teri could hobble around now with the aid of a crude crutch that Estevan had fashioned for him, and he was able to scramble down the trail from the cave without any assistance the night they started southward once again.

With Teri and Jaime astride Galante and Estevan walking in the lead, they could not make nearly as good time as they had with two horses, but they covered a few leagues each night. When they reached the desert at the edge of the Sandia Mountains, with the Manzanos looming ahead of them, Estevan wished desperately that the other horse had not been lost in the avalanche.

This would be the most dangerous part of their journey. They had no cover and the Indians of the Sandias and roving bands of Apaches would be a serious menace. Besides, Estevan was growing increasingly apprehensive about the amount of time they had taken on their journey. What would they do if Lieutenant Governor Garcia had left Isleta? He might be halfway to El Paso del Norte by this time. Estevan had heard tales of the desert south of Isleta. The "Journada del Muerto" (Journey of Death) that stretched thirty leagues without water. How could he and Jaime and Teri ever survive that?

The trail was almost level now and they could move faster. But it was nearly dawn. "We had better look for a place to camp," Estevan said. "It will be dangerous to travel much longer."

"There are rocks up ahead. Perhaps we can hide there," Jaime suggested.

"*Sí.*"

They plodded on. Estevan realized that he was almost too tired to push one foot ahead of the other. He had never thought before about how wearisome it could be to walk league after league. The picture came to his mind of the patient, toiling Indians, with their loads of market goods, who traveled the trails throughout New Mexico respectfully getting out of the way of any Spaniards who flashed by on horseback—and he was ashamed.

His musings were cut short as the huge, menacing figure of an Indian loomed before them in the darkness.

There was no time to flee or take cover. Estevan dropped Galante's reins and stepped back. He looked about frantically, wondering what to do.

The Indian leaped forward with a shout, raising his spear. Before using it, he came close enough to see who the riders were. In the murky light, he apparently did not notice Estevan, seeing only the horse with its double load. He cried out something, brandishing his weapon.

Apache! The worst possible of all Indians! Estevan felt acute terror surge through him and for a moment he had a wild impulse to run. But the Indian's spear poised against his two companions stopped him. He was the only able-bodied one of the trio. As the Apache, recognizing the two riders as enemies, pulled back his arm to hurl the spear, Estevan plunged forward and grappled with him and the spear missed its mark.

"You Called Me Estevan"

Caught off guard by the unexpected attack, the Apache went down with a thud. For a few moments Estevan and the Indian grappled in the sand. Tired and weak from lack of food, however, Estevan knew he was no match for the sinewy muscles of the Apache. He could feel the Indian reaching for his throat.

"Run!" Estevan screamed to the others. "Run!" He tried to claw the Apache's hands away from his neck but his efforts were feeble and ineffective, and the vise began to tighten. Estevan felt as if his eyes would burst from their sockets and his tongue would be forced from his mouth as he gasped, agonizingly, for air.

"Run!" he tried to say again, but the sound was only a feeble croak. And then, as a swirling blackness closed around him, he ceased to struggle.

Slowly, Estevan came up out of the depths of unconsciousness. Someone was rubbing his throat where the pain bound like a rope. Far away, he heard a voice say, "I think he is coming around," and he wondered who was with him. He opened his mouth to breathe more deeply. How wonderful it was to fill his lungs with the crisp morning air! The pain had eased now and he lay with his eyes still closed. Then someone began gently slapping his face.

"Estevan, wake up! You can't sleep all day! Wake up!"

The slapping continued until Estevan was forced to open his eyes. Teri's face was close to his.

"That is better," he said. "We feared you were going to spend the whole morning flat on your back, and Jaime and I are hungry." He grinned.

Estevan struggled to sit up. The sky was a flaming scarlet in the east and the red glow touched the body of the dead Apache that lay nearby, close enough to touch.

Estevan looked at Teri. "You—" he said, his voice thick and strangled, "you called me Estevan."

Teri sat back on his heels and began to laugh. He laughed until he had to wipe the tears from his eyes.

"What is—so funny?" Estevan asked.

"Here I save your life with the best spear throw I have ever made and the only thing you notice is that I called you Estevan!"

"You should have seen it, Senor!" Jaime said, squatting beside the other two. "The Apache was choking the life out of you and I sat there petrified, but Teri hurled his crutch and struck the Indian squarely in the middle of the forehead. And then, before I could move, he leaped from Galante's back and crawled over and sank his knife into the Apache! And there I still sat like a great wooden fool!" He shook his head dismally at the memory of his own ineptitude.

"Don't blame yourself," Teri said cheerfully. "It is a proven fact that the Pueblos are far more intelligent than the Spaniards."

Estevan laughed and the sound caught in his injured throat. "At least, the Pueblo is as conceited as the Spaniard," he said. He looked around. "Do you think there are more Indians?"

Teri shook his head. "This was a messenger, I believe. There are no signs of others. Jaime has searched the rocks ahead and there is nothing."

"Good. Can we hide here?"

172

"Sí."

By nightfall, Estevan had recovered from his brush with death though his throat was swollen and sore. Teri's leg splints, loosened and broken in his plunge from Galante's back, had to be rebound. But his leg seemed miraculously unhurt by the jolt it had taken.

"It is a wonder you did not rebreak the bone," Estevan said as he worked on it.

"It felt, when I landed, as if I had," Teri admitted, "but I didn't have time to think about it."

"I didn't thank you for saving my life," Estevan said.

"It is not necessary. You and I have saved each other so many times now that I have no way of knowing the score."

"And you're both lucky to have me along," Jaime remarked. "Look at the help I've been!"

Estevan clapped him on the shoulder. "We all have our talents," he joked. "Look how well you sit a horse."

Jaime grinned. "I'll do more than that," he promised. "When we get to the Rio Grande, I'll wash all our shirts."

"Do you think they'll need it by then?" Estevan asked, looking down at his dirt-encrusted clothes.

"Need it or not," Teri joined in, "we'll hold him to his promise—if there is water in the Rio Grande."

After a meager breakfast of berries, the boys broke camp and started south once more. They made the next three nights of travel without incident. The going was easy—their one problem was lack of food and water. If it had not been for Teri's knowledge of the desert, they would not have survived. But he knew how to scavenge food and liquid from the cacti and that sustained them.

When at last they topped a rise and saw the dark shadows of Isleta spread out before them in the morning light, Estevan drew a sigh of relief. "We made it," he said. "We finally made it! Do you think it safe to go down openly?"

Teri shook his head. "I do not know for sure," he replied. "Isleta refused to join the rebellion, but they could have been attacked by Apaches and driven out. It looks too quiet down there."

Again, Teri's judgment was correct. There was no sign of life, though at this time of day, people should have been about. No women could be seen building fires, no dogs barked, no children were crying.

"We had best approach with caution," Estevan said.

"Let me go in first and look around," Jaime suggested.

"No, if the Apaches are here, we have probably already been seen," Teri said. "One would have less chance than three."

Slowly, they approached the village that sprawled along the banks of the Rio Grande, the Manzano Mountains looming purple and blue in the distance.

"Look," Jaime pointed. "The church has been burned!"

The adobe walls of the church were still standing but they had been blackened by fire and the boys could see where the roof beams had burned and fallen inward. No one said anything more, but the boys feared what they would find.

They passed one of the great ash piles that marked the four corners of the pueblo and walked slowly toward the central plaza. Passing the church and the kivas, they could see beyond the buildings of the Spanish settlement. Some seemed to be in ruins, others stood untouched. But there was no sign of life. They peered into some of the buildings. Everything was completely deserted.

At last the boys stopped and looked at each other, facing the grim truth. Isleta was abandoned! They faced the Journada del Muerto alone!

12

"I, Too, Shall Be Tending the Seed"

For a moment, no one spoke. The hot sun beat down on their heads and, from somewhere, a mockingbird sang.

"Perhaps we can overtake them," Estevan said, breaking the silence. "There will be women and children. They cannot travel fast."

"Yes," Teri agreed. "Perhaps we can." He looked around. "I wonder if the Indians all went with them, or if they have fled."

"Whatever happened, they are certainly gone," Jaime remarked.

"We had better look around. There might be some food somewhere," Teri suggested.

The boys made a systematic search of each building and were rewarded by finding a sack of grain, a welcome discovery for Galante, and two baskets of maize. They also found several water bottles.

"These will help," Teri said, looking at their treasure, "but they won't take us through the Journada."

"That doesn't start for another five or ten leagues," Jaime said.

"No, we will have a chance to gather some food and re-fill our water containers before we reach it," Teri agreed.

"And God willing, we will overtake the others before we get to the Journada," Estevan added.

The Rio Grande was dry but there were muddy stretches and by digging in them, the boys found the streams which ran underground at that time of the year.

"Too bad we don't want to take time to hold Jaime to his promise about washing our shirts," Estevan remarked wryly as they packed their meager supplies on Galante.

"*Si*, but I am afraid that it may be only the dirt that is holding them together," Teri said soberly. "If that were washed out, they might fall apart."

"Well, I offered," Jaime said virtuously. "I did my part, whether you accept or not."

"He probably knew he was safe when he made the offer," Estevan said, smiling.

He turned back to his horse. "Ah, Galante, you never expected to be a pack horse, did you?" he asked, patting the animal. "And what a sight you are!"

The stallion did, indeed, show the effects of the rough journey from Taos. His once-shining, black coat was dull and patchy and burrs matted the silky mane. As the horse whinnied and tossed his head, Estevan thought of the terrible journey ahead and wondered dismally if Galante could survive the ordeal. Well, there was no guarantee that any of them could, for that matter.

The boys resumed their journey, with Teri astride Galante, and Jaime and Estevan walking alongside. They traveled in silence, following the Rio Grande, and were grateful for the shade of the cottonwood trees whose balls of fluff filled the air with drifting white seeds.

"Senor Estevan—" Jaime began, but he was interrupted by Teri.

"Ah," the Indian said, addressing no one in particular, "how hard the old ways die with the Spaniard. An Indian rides while the ranchero walks, but his servant is still his servant."

"What do you mean?" Estevan asked.

Teri grinned down at him. "I, a poor downtrodden Pueblo, have come to call you Estevan, but your fellow Spaniard must call you Senor."

Estevan laughed and realized that a few weeks ago, he would have been greatly offended by Teri's remark. "He need not call me Senor ever again," he said, looking at Jaime. "When I can't even get him to wash my shirt, I guess I can't consider him a servant."

"So now I call him Estevan," Jaime said, "and when the rebellion is put down, I starve to death because I am no longer his man. *Gracias*, Teri. You are a big help!"

"When the rebellion is over, you and I may starve together," Estevan said slowly. "Things will never be the same."

"We may all three starve together, even before the rebellion is over," Teri interjected.

"He is truly a comfort to have along, is he not, Sen—" Jaime began, then quickly corrected himself with, "Estevan?"

Estevan nodded. "I'm beginning to wonder why I didn't leave him bogged down in the avalanche!"

"I, Too, Shall Be Tending the Seed"

The trail along the Rio Grande was easy to travel and the boys made good progress. They kept a sharp eye out for Indians but saw no sign of any, and when they finally stopped for the night, they felt more cheerful over their prospects of overtaking the refugees from Isleta. There was some evidence of them along the way and it was fresh enough to make them feel that Lieutenant Governor Garcia and his people were not more than a few days ahead of them.

At last the day came when they could see, curling against the gray sky of dusk, the smoke of campfires.

"There they are!" Estevan cried excitedly. He began to run, all weariness forgotten, the answer to the terrible gnawing anxiety about his people close at hand. Then suddenly, he stopped.

"What is it?" Jaime asked, hurrying over to him. "Why did you stop?"

"I'm afraid," Estevan said slowly. "I'm afraid of what we'll find."

For a moment, no one spoke.

"I know that some of your people escaped from Santa Fe," Teri said finally. "Perhaps you will be fortunate and find all of your family up ahead."

"Yes, perhaps." But Estevan did not run again. The three approached the refugee camp slowly. Challenged by a guard at the outskirts of the camp, they stopped. The man, a bearded soldier wearing a leather helmet and carrying a harquebus, looked them over.

"Are you from Santa Fe?" he asked.

"Yes, but by way of Taos," Estevan said. "I am Estevan Algadonez. Are there other Santa Fe refugees with you?"

The soldier shook his head. "Not yet. The governor got

word that there's a group of them over near Socorro. He's gone
to see. That's why we've been camped here for four days."
He scowled up at Teri.

"Since when do Indians ride while Spaniards walk?"
he asked roughly.

"Since they are my friends and are injured," Estevan
said evenly. "May we pass?"

"Not with him on the horse," the guard said flatly.

"It is all right," Teri said, preparing to slide down. "I
can go the rest of the way with my crutch."

"No! Stay where you are!" Estevan's voice was suddenly shrill as he fought to control the anger welling up in
him. The issue seemed a strangely important one to him. Who
was this lout of a mercenary to stand in his way with such
orders? Did he not know what the rebellion was all about?
He spoke to the soldier, and his voice crackled with authority.

"You will let us pass or I shall see the governor when he
returns and complain of your insolence!"

In spite of himself, the soldier was awed by Estevan's
outburst. The young man had an air about him—there was
no question of that. Maybe he was someone important. But,
by the saints, he didn't know what this rebellion was all
about if he let an Indian ride his horse! The soldier shrugged
and stepped back. It wasn't worth making a row over. The
world was falling apart anyway, so what difference did it
make?

Reaching the camp, Estevan's first impression was one
of complete disorder and apathy. He had difficulty locating
the officer in charge and when he did, the man seemed completely indifferent to their plight.

"We are looking for the governor in a few more days,"

he said. "Build your fires where you will. You have to furnish your own food." With that, he turned back to the dice game which Estevan had interrupted.

The situation seemed increasingly alarming to Estevan as he looked around. He had thought that once they reached other Spaniards, their troubles would be over. But as he looked at the dull faces of the refugees, the indifferent soldiers and the sullen Indians, he wondered if they would not have a better chance trying the Journada by themselves.

Weary and dispirited, he made his way back to where he had left his two friends. "I hope things are better when the governor gets here," he said. "Maybe Otérmin can put some order into this group."

"We know where the Isleta Indians are," Teri said, nodding toward the Indian camp at one side. "One told me that Garcia forced most of them to come along. He probably needed them to carry things."

"Yes," Estevan agreed heavily, "he probably did."

That day and the next were the longest two that Estevan had ever endured. Ever since he had been captured, there had been in the back of his mind an oppressive fear for his people at Santa Fe, but problems of survival on the trail had been too immediate and pressing, and he had been too exhausted each morning to brood over his anxieties.

Now, sitting in the hot sun of the desert and listening to the wails of cranky children and the wrangling of the soldiers, Estevan could not keep from thinking about what might have taken place back at the capital. His thoughts dwelt on all the terrible things that could have happened, until he felt he would go mad. He busied himself helping Jaime and Teri make their little camp, scavenging about for any material he could find for fires and helping to set snares for jackrabbits and prairie dogs. But there was still not enough to do. A dozen times, during those weary days, he rode Galante north as far as he dared, searching the flat, dun-colored desert for any sign of the approaching party.

At last, late in the afternoon of the second day, he could see a small cloud of dust against the horizon. He watched intently. Was it a band of Apaches or pursuing Pueblos? People in camp said they had seen Indians lurking about from time to time. But the group was moving too slowly to be Indians. Then Estevan caught a flash of the Spanish flag in the waning sunlight. He spurred Galante forward. There was no hanging back this time. His fear of what he would learn was swallowed up in his need to know.

Estevan's heart pounded as he approached the straggling caravan. He strained his eyes to try to pick out his loved ones before he was even close enough to distinguish one person from another. The first people in the group were soldiers, then came several carretas carrying the wounded and infirm. Estevan scanned these fearfully, not knowing whether he was relieved or even more frightened when he did not see any of his own family or friends in them.

After the carts came the people, hundreds of them. Tired, dirty and with the same apathetic look of the Isleta refugees, they plodded along, their eyes on the hot sand beneath their feet. Slowly, Estevan rode through the group of straggling people, his heart growing heavier each moment. Then suddenly, he heard his name called.

"Estevan! Estevan Algadonez, is that you?"

He turned to locate the voice and realized that he had ridden past Juan Otéro without recognizing him. Leaping from Galante's back, he embraced his friend.

"I should have known you'd turn up!" Juan said, holding him off and looking at him, his eyes shining.

"And you," Estevan said. "The Pueblos would be no match for you. But my family—are they—?"

"Yes," Juan said. "They are here—at the rear. Your mother, she has trouble keeping up."

"They are all right?"

"Yes, as right as any of us. The sight of you will do wonders for them."

"*Gracias.* I'll talk to you later."

Eagerly, Estevan made his way to the rear of the slowly moving group, searching each face as he passed. When he saw his parents his joy was tempered. Unthinkingly, he had expected them to look as they had when he left them. But the two figures trailing behind the rest of the refugees bore only a faint resemblance to the erect and proud pair he had left at the Casa Real a few weeks before. Their clothes were torn and gray with dust. Doña Magdalena's hair straggled out from under a dirty *rebozo* (shawl) draped over her head. Her shoes were flapping as she walked, the stitching torn by many miles of wear. Both figures seemed small and bent. They did not look up and Don Ramon's arm supported his wife as they walked. To Estevan, watching, it seemed as if each feeble step were an agony of achievement.

Estevan's eyes filled with tears. He dropped Galante's reins and held out his hands. "Mother!" he said. "Father!"

The two weary refugees looked up. All at once, Doña

183

Magdalena's weathered face crumpled into myriad wrinkles as she burst into tears.

"My son!" she sobbed. "Oh, my son!"

Estevan's strong young arms enveloped his parents and all three were alternately weeping and laughing in the knowledge that they were all alive and together again.

The arrival of Governor Otérmin and the refugees from Santa Fe put new heart into the Isleta group. God had performed a miracle in helping Otérmin break through the besieging Pueblos. And did that not mean that they would manage to get through the Journada, also? Those gathered for Father Andres' evening services were full of gratitude and hope as they bowed their heads in prayer.

Most grateful of all was the Algadonez family, and the gaiety around its campfire later was contagious as friends came by to express their joy at Estevan's escape and to hear his story. Even Governor Otérmin, busy as he was, took time to embrace Estevan and tell him he was grateful for his escape.

When Estevan blamed himself for the failure of his mission, the governor said, "It is of no matter. You tried your best—and we have survived."

There had been one strained moment when the Otéros came: Isabella, her skin burned and peeling from the sun, her hair thick with dust, but still lovely, Senor and Senora Otéro and Juan. Estevan had greeted them and asked, "But where is Felipe? Is he on guard duty?"

There had been an awkward moment of silence, then Estevan realized the answer to his question. "I—I am sorry," he said. "I did not think. He—he was killed?"

184

Senor Otéro nodded sadly.

"*Si*," Juan said heavily, "an arrow through the neck the last day of the siege."

Poor little Felipe, Estevan thought solemnly, so quiet, so good-natured—dead before he had had a chance to live. "I'm sorry," he said again, his words stupidly inadequate in his ears.

"But we thank God for His blessings," Senora Otéro said quietly. "He has spared us our other children."

"Your son and his family at the hacienda escaped?" Estevan asked.

"*Si*. And that, too, was a miracle," Senora Otéro said.

"There were many miracles," Juan added soberly. The expression in his friend's eyes told Estevan that Juan Otéro would never again be the carefree boy he had once been.

"Was it a terrible battle, when you left Santa Fe?" Estevan asked.

"No, they did not attack at all," Juan replied. "We simply opened the doors of the Casa Real and filed out. The soldiers divided to defend the front and rear of the columns of refugees. Everyone carried what he could."

"We were all prepared to die fighting, if necessary," Senora Otéro said. "But there was no attack, thank God."

"Why didn't they attack?" Estevan asked. "Surely, that would have been the time. With so many women and children, the soldiers could not have begun to save them."

Don Ramon spoke. "Governor Otérmin thinks it was because our soldiers fought so gallantly the day before. In the foray against the Indians that day, our men killed over three hundred of their warriors."

"And you weren't attacked at all on the journey south?"

"No," Juan said. "We expected an attack momentarily, but none came. There was an ambush planned south of Sandia, but our scouts discovered it and only a few shots were exchanged."

Estevan shook his head. "It is incredible. How many escaped?"

"Over one thousand," Juan replied.

"Do you suppose that the Pueblos only want to be free of us and that they have no desire to kill any more than is necessary?" Estevan asked, thinking of Teri.

The usually mild-mannered Senor Otéro spoke now. He spat out his words with a venom which surprised Estevan. "Not those cowardly, murdering devils!" he blurted. "They would shoot a boy through the neck but they've no stomach for a fight when they are outnumbered, even if only by women and children!"

Senora Otéro stood up. "You are forgetting that God was on our side," she said firmly. "The matter needs no more explanation than that. Come, we must get back to our own fire or that lazy Maria will let it go out."

Estevan smiled faintly as he watched them go. Neither hardship nor tragedy could destroy the sense of authority that emanated from Senora Otéro's proud figure. And Senorita Isabella—he had nearly forgotten the beauty of that face and figure, and the enchanting way she had of lowering her lashes over those lovely, dark eyes. Ah, life was good, he thought, in spite of rebellion and dangers and deprivation.

He looked at his own family, now gathered around the campfire. Jaime was helping Doña Magdalena to another piece of broiled rabbit, and Don Ramon was adding a bit of wood to the fire. But where was Teri? Estevan realized that he had not seen the Indian boy since he had brought in the jackrabbit all skinned and ready to be cooked.

"Has anyone seen Teri?" Estevan asked.

Jaime looked around. "No, he disappeared just before supper."

"He's probably over there with the other Pueblos," Don Ramon said, nodding toward the Isleta encampment.

"He should be *here*," Estevan said. "I'll find him."

"If he has not already eaten, have him come and eat of our food," Don Ramon said graciously. "I have not had the occasion to do so yet, but I would like to thank him for many things."

It was almost an hour before Estevan located his friend. Teri was nowhere to be found among the other Indians, but at last Estevan saw a solitary figure sitting on a boulder some distance from the hissing campfires. He was a lonely figure, silhouetted against the deepening gray of the sky.

"Why did you not eat with us?" Estevan asked bluntly.

Teri turned his head. "I was not hungry," he said.

"The food was yours. You should have had some. Come back with me now and eat."

Teri shook his head.

"At least come back to the fire. The night will be cold."

"I have spent many cold nights without a fire," the Indian replied.

"And I, too," Estevan said, "but I certainly don't intend to do it again unless I have to. Come." He held out his hand.

"Ah, Estevan, you will not see what you do not wish to

see," Teri said, ignoring the hand. "We are no longer on the trail. We are among your people, and you are a Spaniard and I am an Indian. Why do you fight the truth?"

"Because it isn't the truth," Estevan said stubbornly. "It is you who will not see. We are not Indian and Spaniard. We are brothers."

"Perhaps you and I know that we are brothers, but your parents would not see it, nor would your friends. I could come to your campfire as your servant, but not as your equal."

Estevan remembered Senor Otéro's bitter words. And even Don Ramon's, "I would thank him for many things," had a ring of condescension.

"Our people are too different in their ways and their thoughts. The old hatreds—and the new—" Teri did not finish his sentence.

There was silence for a few minutes. The stars, huge and close in the New Mexican sky, blinked down upon the two boys.

Estevan sighed. "If you and I cannot prove the brotherhood we have learned, then God help our country, for there can never be true peace," he said sadly. "There will be only master and servant."

"You Spaniards!" Teri said, and there was a hint of laughter in his voice. "It is all or nothing with you. Because you cannot make all of New Mexico see at once the lesson we have learned so painfully, you see only failure."

"What do you mean?" Estevan asked.

"I mean that we have come to understand each other and that is a beginning. I'll never hate all Spaniards again as I did, and you'll never hate all Indians. And there are others like us among our peoples. Perhaps in time we who do not hate will prevail."

Estevan shook his head. "It will take so long," he sighed.

Teri laughed. "There you are, all impatience still," he said. "We Pueblos know that patience is a part of life. It is a long time between planting and harvest but we are planting the seed, you and I, and if we tend it carefully, those who come after us will enjoy the harvest."

Estevan held out his hand again to his friend. "All right," he said, grinning at Teri, "I'll go back to my people and become the best farmer in New Mexico!"

This time, Teri accepted Estevan's gesture and their hands met. "Not the best," he said, "for I, too, shall be tending the seed."

Estevan laughed. "Then I shall be one of the best," he conceded.

Author's Note

The terrible march through the Journada del Muerto which followed the joining of the Isleta and Santa Fe refugees is one of the most harrowing of retreats in all of history. The journey took nine days and of the two thousand five hundred and twenty refugees who started, only one thousand nine hundred and forty-seven survived.

There were fifty deaths per day—a grave for every thousand feet of desert traversed. Where possible, the dying were carried along to the next campsite, where the priests would hold a Requiem High Mass for all.

At the southern end of the Journada, the refugees met a relief column that had been sent out in answer to a courier Lieutenant Governor Garcia had sent to El Paso. After that, there was food and water for the suffering Spaniards.

The Spaniards continued their retreat until they reached a point about twelve miles from the present city of El Paso.

There, they built themselves a temporary encampment. That "temporary" settlement was the home of the refugees for twelve long years until the expedition of Vargas, sent out from Mexico City, succeeded in leading the Spaniards back up into New Mexico.

Vargas met with very little resistance from the Pueblos who had wearied of the tyranny of El Popé and had come to realize that without the Spaniards, their economy was ruined.

Out of the Great Rebellion came the realization by both sides of their mutual need for each other and, even more importantly, of a mutual respect for one another. The Spaniard was never again quite so arrogant and the Pueblo was never again quite so bitter. There was no sudden flowering of understanding and warm friendliness, but there was a new tolerance which had been paid for dearly in human suffering.

—Helen Lobdell
Benton Harbor, Michigan

Sources Consulted

Fergusson, Erna
    New Mexico: A Pageant of Three Peoples
    Alfred Knopf, N.Y., 1955
Forbes, Jack D.
    Apache, Navaho and Spaniard
    University of Oklahoma Press, Norman, 1960
Hallenbeck, Cleve, and Williams, Juanita H.
    Legends of the Southwest
    Arthur H. Clark and Company, Glendale, 1938
Horgan, Paul
    Conquistadores in North American History
    Farrar, Strauss and Company, N.Y., 1963
Lummis, Charles F.
    The Land of Poco Tiempo
    University of New Mexico Press
    Albuquerque, 1952
Miller and Alsberg, Eds.
    New Mexico: A Guide to a Colorful State
    Federal Writers Project, New Mexico
    Hastings House, N.Y., 1953
Stanley, F.
    Cuidad Santa Fe: 1610–1821
    World Press Inc., Denver, 1958
Warren, Nona Otero
    Old Spain in Our Southwest
    Rio Grande Press, Chicago, 1962